"Are You Going To Walk Out Of My Life?"

Faith asked abruptly.

Jones shoved his thumbs into the pockets of his jeans. "I don't want to, but I have to."

"Why?"

"Because it's best that way. You have to understand. Please don't ask me—"

"I *don't* understand, and I *will* ask you, dammit." She flung the sleeping bag aside and rounded on him. "And I'll keep on asking until you tell me. I can be just as stubborn as you." She folded her arms across her breasts and stared at him.

He smiled wistfully. "I have no doubt."

When he offered nothing more, she knew this was a lost cause. He had no right to kiss her like that and then walk out of her life without a word, but he was going to do it anyway.

Dear Reader,

You can tell from the presence of some *very* handsome hunks on the covers that something special is going on for Valentine's Day here at Silhouette Desire! That "something" is a group of guys we call "Bachelor Boys"... you know, those men who think they'll never get "caught" by a woman—until they do! They're our very special Valentine's Day gift to you.

The lineup is pretty spectacular: a *Man of the Month* by Ann Major, and five other fabulous books by Raye Morgan, Peggy Moreland, Karen Leabo, Audra Adams and a *brand-new* to Silhouette author, Susan Carroll. You won't be able to pick up just one! So, you'll have to buy all six of these delectable, sexy stories.

Next month, we have even more fun in store: a *Man of the Month* from the sizzling pen of Jackie Merritt, a delicious story by Joan Johnston, and four more wonderful Desire love stories.

So read ... and enjoy ... as these single guys end up *happily* tamed by the women of their dreams.

Until next month,

Lucia Macro
Senior Editor

Please address questions and book requests to:
Reader Service
U.S.: P.O. Box 1325, Buffalo, NY 14269
Canadian: P.O. Box 1050, Niagara Falls, Ont. L2E 7G7

KAREN LEABO

TWILIGHT MAN

SILHOUETTE *Desire*®

Published by Silhouette Books

America's Publisher of Contemporary Romance

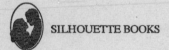 SILHOUETTE BOOKS

ISBN 0-373-05838-1

TWILIGHT MAN

Copyright © 1994 by Karen Leabo

Books by Karen Leabo

Silhouette Desire

Close Quarters #629
Lindy and the Law #676
Unearthly Delights #704
The Cop #767
Ben #794
Feathers and Lace #824
Twilight Man #838

Silhouette Romance

Roses Have Thorns #648
Ten Days in Paradise #692
Domestic Bliss #707
Full Bloom #731
Smart Stuff #764
Runaway Bride #797
The Housewarming #848
A Changed Man #866

KAREN LEABO

credits her fourth-grade teacher with initially sparking her interest in creative writing. She was determined at an early age to have her work published. When she was in the eighth grade, she wrote a children's book and convinced her school yearbook publisher to put it in print.

Karen was born and raised in Dallas. She has worked as a magazine art director, a free-lance writer and a textbook editor, but now she keeps herself busy full-time writing about romance.

Prologue

Dusk fell early on that dismal March day. Already aggravated and way behind schedule, Faith Kimball flipped on her car lights and peered intently through the windshield for some sign of the turnoff that would lead her to the campgrounds.

Every motel within casting distance of Caddo Lake was full this weekend, thanks to some fishing tournament. At least she'd brought her camping supplies with her on this trip, although she wasn't looking forward to pitching a tent and fixing dinner in the dark.

Black Cypress Campgrounds was supposed to be three or four miles down FM 23, according to the manager at the last motel she'd tried. But, dammit, she'd driven four miles already and she hadn't seen—no, wait a minute. What did that sign say?

She slowed way down as she approached the faded,

peeling sign, which was hung too high for her headlights to illuminate. Yes, that was it!

Her triumph was short-lived. She looked up to see a huge dump truck barreling toward her at an alarming speed. His headlights were off, and he was driving dead center down the narrow, two-lane blacktop road.

Several thoughts flashed lightning fast through her mind. My God, didn't the idiot see her? She should honk. She should veer off the road and take her chances in the ditch. She did neither when it seemed the truck would miss her after all. Then it swerved and slammed head-on into her compact car without ever hitting the brakes.

Faith's car folded in on itself as it spun around and around, then rolled end over end like a nightmarish carnival ride. She was conscious of her head striking the windshield and a pressure against her left thigh, but there was no pain.

She wondered if she was about to die. Oddly, that idea didn't frighten her. She felt only a few regrets—that she hadn't married or had children, that she hadn't told her mother goodbye, and that her doctoral dissertation would go unfinished. Then she felt nothing.

A voice brought Faith back through a dark curtain. "Wake up, dammit. Unfasten your seat belt! Lady, I know you're alive. Wake *up!*"

Unable to disobey, she opened her eyes. *Now* she felt the pain and the fear. Her clothes were soaked with blood, and her lungs were filled with smoke. She coughed and tasted more blood.

Oh, God, she didn't want to die!

"Unfasten your seat belt," the commanding voice said again.

Although the effort cost her, she did what he asked.

"Give me your hand." Now that he had her attention, the voice was gentler.

There was a whoosh of heat as something nearby caught fire. Closing her eyes against the blinding, stinging smoke, Faith reached out.

Strong hands caught hers in a crushing grip. She bit her lip to keep from screaming from the pain as he pulled her up or sideways—she wasn't sure which way was up anymore.

"That's it, almost there," he crooned as the crumbled safety glass from a shattered window scraped her bare legs. As soon as she was free of the twisted metal that had once been her car, her rescuer clutched her against his chest and ran like hell.

Moments later a deafening explosion sent them both flying. As they hit the ground, the blow knocked the breath out of her—what little breath was left. Her world went black.

She awoke to the strange feel of her rescuer's hard mouth on hers, breathing life-giving air into her lungs. She pushed him away, coughing from the thick black smoke she'd inhaled, but breathing on her own.

"Thank God," he muttered. "Just relax. Help is coming. I flagged a car down, and the driver called from his mobile phone." As he spoke in low, reassuring tones, his strong but gentle hands probed for injuries.

She opened her stinging eyes just once so that she could see what he looked like. As he removed a headband of some sort, she got only a fleeting impression of longish, dark hair and deep-set eyes, a straight nose and a square chin with a cleft.

He tied the headband around her upper thigh.

"Hurts," she mumbled.

"I know it hurts, darlin'," he said, brushing a lock of her curly blond hair from her face. "Hear that siren? Help is here." Then he stood and walked away.

"Wait. Wait!" she called out with the last bit of strength she had in her. "Don't leave me! Who are you?"

He never broke stride.

One

As the April day dawned warm and clear, Jones Larabee had nothing more pressing on his mind than whether to go fishing or simply work on his tan. Nothing, that is, until he looked out the window of his cabin and spied Miss Hildy's canoe heading toward him through the swamp.

He wondered how she kept from tipping over. She was wider than the boat, which sometimes wobbled alarmingly. But she always managed to deftly maneuver the canoe to shore without mishap.

Jones went down to meet her. Although she was meddlesome and tended to hover over him worse than any mother hen, he liked Hildy. A descendant of the Caddo Indians who had settled in the area centuries ago, Hildy was known as the local medicine woman. Some people disliked her, others feared her, but everyone on both sides of the Texas-Louisiana state line respected her knowledge of the swamp and its flora and fauna.

"Howdy, Jones," she said as she heaved herself over the edge of the canoe and waded in the last few feet, soaking her ragged, much-patched tennis shoes.

"Mornin'." He grabbed the boat's bow and eased it onto the muddy shore. "What brings you here? It's not your usual day to come calling."

"A body doesn't have to have a reason to call on a friend, does she?" Hildy reached into the canoe and retrieved two large plastic buckets, in which were stored a variety of treasures from her vast garden. "'Sides, with all this rain we've had, my early crops are already out of control. I've got to get rid of this produce somehow. I can't sell it all at the stand."

Jones relieved her of the heavy buckets. "I haven't finished what you gave me last week."

"Then you're not eating enough greens," she scolded. "What about the tea? You're drinking my special tea, aren't you?"

"Yeah, yeah. I'm almost out."

"Then it's a good thing I came today," she said as they headed toward Jones's rough-hewn pine cabin, dwarfed by the towering cypress, pine and oak trees surrounding it. "I brought you a big jar."

Months ago, when Jones had first come here, Hildy had sniffed him out like a bird dog hunting quail. She just wanted to have a look-see at her closest neighbor, she'd claimed, but Jones doubted that. He didn't know where she lived—somewhere deep in the swamp, where a man could get lost and wander for days—but he didn't think it was anywhere close to him. She was just nosy.

Since her first visit, she had paddled to his island once a week, whether he'd invited her or not. Eventually he'd found himself charmed by her backwoods philosophy and her no-nonsense approach to life, and he now counted her as a friend.

His only friend. None of the other locals came near his cabin, and that was fine with him.

A chair in Jones's kitchen creaked as Hildy plopped down in it. "I really did come for another reason," she said, watching Jones where he stood at the sink washing the greens she'd brought. "There's a gal lookin' for you."

His whole body stiffened. "Who is she?" But who else could it be except Mary-Lynn?

He had taken precautions so that no one from his old life could follow him here. He hadn't applied for a driver's license or even a post office box. He didn't have a telephone. He had left his car behind, so there were no license plates to trace. His boat, which had come with the cabin rental, wasn't registered in his name. How could anyone have found him?

"Pretty little thing," Hildy said. "Blond curls all over."

Jones allowed himself to relax. Not Mary-Lynn, then, whose hair was almost as black as Hildy's.

"I saw her at Pete's," Hildy continued. "She had that old green bandanna of yours. The thing's in pieces, and she was showin' it around to everyone in the store, trying to find someone who could tell her who it belonged to."

He allowed himself a smile. "Ah, then I know who she is." The blonde had to be the hit-and-run victim he'd pulled from the burning car several weeks ago. He'd been tromping around in the woods, minding his own business, when he'd heard the crash on the road just a few yards away. Although he didn't like involving himself in other people's problems, he could hardly have ignored a life-and-death situation.

He had applied hasty first aid to the woman, enough to get her by until the paramedics arrived. As soon as they did, he'd hightailed it out of there. He didn't need some strange woman's undying gratitude for saving her life.

"You didn't say anything to her, did you?" he asked Hildy.

"No. I know how you like your privacy."

He could see she was brimming with curiosity, but he declined to tell her the story. He didn't feel much like a hero, and he didn't want anyone thinking of him that way.

With promises to drink his tea and eat his greens, he hurried Hildy on her way. He knew she needed to open up her roadside produce stand, which provided her only income—she wouldn't accept any money for the vegetables she brought him.

When she was gone, his thoughts returned to the angel-faced woman who had been so near death, her skin as white as an egret's feather. He was glad to hear she had recovered. But he hoped like hell she didn't find him.

Faith studied the crude map the campgrounds manager had drawn for her, then peered at the scene ahead. This wasn't the first time she'd tracked down someone who lived in an area so remote that she had to follow landmarks rather than street names or house numbers. This was, however, the first time she'd attempted to do it in a swamp from a leaky dinghy with a balky outboard motor.

Ahead of her loomed a huge cypress tree, cleaved down the middle as if a giant's ax had split it. She recognized it as one of her landmarks. "Struck by lightnin'," Hoady had said. With a mild pang of apprehension she turned off the clearly marked "lake road" and onto a much narrower channel, slowing her speed in deference to the submerged logs and other hazards that lurked just below the water's surface.

Fortunately, the channel wasn't hard to follow. A definite path wended its way through the water lilies, as if another boat had recently passed. She settled back and tried to relax.

Over the past few months while working on her dissertation she had learned to enjoy the sights and sounds of the swamp, the strange creatures, the earthy smells and the people who lived here—especially the people. They were a breed unto themselves. Judging from Jones Larabee's eccentric reputation, he was a prime example. She couldn't wait to meet him.

The campgrounds manager, Hoady Fromme, had tried to talk her out of going to see Larabee. He'd said the man was spooky, a loner and a mean one at that. But Faith only half believed what Hoady told her. Country people, she had discovered, were prone to exaggeration when they met her and noticed she was enthralled with their every word. And anyway, a man who risked his own life to save hers couldn't be all bad.

At the very least, she would give Mr. Larabee the new bandanna she'd bought him and thank him for saving her life. At best, she would get him talking and convince him to let her videotape him. An interview with the local hermit would make a nice addition to her dissertation. He might be one of the last bastions of local folklore and superstitions, which were dying out as civilization encroached.

Faith spotted the next landmark, a vast "field" of water lilies on her left. Later in the summer those huge lily pads would produce impressive, waxy white flowers as big as dinner plates. From there she turned into an even smaller channel, slowing the motor further until she barely putted along, ducking under tendrils of Spanish moss that dangled from low branches.

She had never been to such a dense part of the swamp.
The dimness pressed in on her, and the sounds made by
creatures on the bank no longer seemed friendly. She had
an overwhelming urge to flee back into the sunlight, but
unless she wanted to flee in reverse, she would have to find
a wider place to turn the boat around.

The idea of backing out was sounding better all the time
when, unexpectedly, the channel widened into a sunlit area
of open water. And in the middle of that water a tiny spit
of land protruded, on which sat one of the prettiest little
houses Faith had ever seen.

The steep-roofed, pine log cabin, which stood on tall
stilts, featured an inviting wraparound porch. Faith could
easily imagine sitting in a rocking chair on that porch with
a cold glass of lemonade, watching the sun set. The neatly
maintained yard was dotted with carefully sculpted cedar
trees. Geraniums, blooming in a profusion of pink and
white, were grouped around the staircase that led to the
front door. A pair of woodpeckers darted back and forth
to a bird feeder hanging from one of the trees.

The storybook image didn't look anything like the
weathered, broken-down hermit's shack she had anticipated. If this wasn't Jones Larabee's home, perhaps the
residents could direct her to where he lived.

Faith nosed her dinghy onto the shore and climbed out.
After tying the boat to a stump, she climbed the steps to the
front door and raised her fist, intending to knock briskly.

She didn't get the chance. The door opened abruptly and
the man coming out nearly plowed her over. When he
backed up a couple of paces, clearly stunned to find a
strange woman on his front porch, she could see he carried
a fishing pole in one hand, a tackle box in the other, and he
wore nothing but a skimpy pair of cut-off jeans.

"Who are you?" he barked as he dropped the tackle box with a thud. "What are you doing here?"

That voice. She couldn't be mistaken. In anger, the timbre of this man's voice was identical to the one she remembered ordering her to unfasten her seat belt. Although she couldn't recall much about his face, the voice had stuck in her mind. Mostly, though, she remembered the gentleness.

He sounded far from gentle now.

Well accustomed to the sometimes ornery resistance she encountered from the people around here when they were confronted by an outsider, she flashed her most winning smile. "I'm Faith Kimball, Mr. Larabee. I came to give you this." She held out a brand-new, bright green bandanna. "I bought it to replace the one you used to bandage my leg. The paramedic had to cut it off—the bandanna, not my leg," she said with a nervous laugh as she realized she was babbling.

The man continued to stare at her with undisguised hostility. "Lady, have you lost your mind?"

For the first time she wondered if she might possibly be mistaken. "You're Jones Larabee, aren't you?"

"No."

The response was quick, defensive—and a lie. Faith had studied human behavior enough that she was very good at spotting lies. She briefly studied his face. He looked about right—the dark brown hair that reached almost to his shoulders, deep-set hazel eyes, a long, straight nose and a square chin with a cleft.

And a gorgeous torso. Naturally she hadn't noticed that when she'd thought she was dying, but she sure noticed it now.

"Then you're not the man who pulled me from my car after a truck hit it down on FM 23?" she asked carefully. "I could swear you're the same man."

His gaze flickered lower, then back up. He'd seen the scar on her leg, she was sure. "You're mistaken," he said coolly. "Now would you mind leaving?"

Pushing Hoady's warnings to the back of her mind, she persisted. She pulled the genuine item—the ragged, faded bandanna—still stained slightly with her blood—from her pocket. "You don't recognize this?"

"Lady, if you don't get off my property—"

"Oh, I get it. You're afraid I'll sue you or something. You don't have to worry about that. The doctor who patched me up said you undoubtedly saved my life with the tourniquet and the mouth-to-mouth resuscitation."

Finally he showed her something besides anger. As if remembering those tense moments when he had breathed life back into her body, his expression turned pensive, and he moistened his lower lip with the tip of his tongue. Still, he didn't admit that he was her rescuer.

Discouraged, she decided she had no choice but to retreat gracefully. The man had his right to privacy. She thrust the new bandanna into his hand. "Take this, anyway," she said. "The color brings out the green in your eyes." Before he could object, she turned and descended the stairs. As she returned to her boat, she felt the heat of his glare on the back of her neck.

Strange man, she thought as she pushed the dinghy into the water and climbed in. Her overdeveloped sense of curiosity made her wonder what set of circumstances led to his forsaking society to live alone in the swamp. Or perhaps she was awarding more melodrama to the situation than it warranted. Maybe this was the only society he knew.

She grabbed the outboard motor's starter cord and gave it a pull. The engine growled weakly but didn't start. She gripped the handle for another pull, this one with more muscle. The results weren't encouraging.

Determined, she knelt on the plank seat in the back of the boat, put both hands on the starter, and yanked for all she was worth. This time the rope broke and she tumbled over the edge of the dinghy onto her rear in two feet of muddy water.

It wouldn't have been so bad, if she hadn't had an audience. But as she sat there in the muck, she could see Jones Larabee, all six-foot-plus of him, standing at the bottom of the stairs watching her with undeniable amusement on his face.

"Problems?" he asked innocently.

She almost let her temper get the best of her. But before she could make a rude retort, one he richly deserved, her common sense intervened. Maybe the Fates were giving her a second chance with the moody Mr. Larabee.

"It appears the motor isn't working," she said as she stood and tried to wipe the mud off her shorts and her legs with the remnants of his old bandanna. "Guess I'll have to paddle back. Unless . . . Do you know how to fix it?"

He shook his head, but he did come closer. "Other than adding gas, I don't know anything about boat motors."

That was odd, she thought. Any man who'd grown up on these waters would surely know all there was to know about boats.

"Where'd you get this piece of junk, anyway?" he asked.

"I rented it from the Black Cypress Campgrounds."

He nodded his understanding. "Hoady. That explains it." He didn't elaborate.

"Any suggestions?" she asked.

After a moment of consideration, he seemed to make a decision. "I was on my way out fishing. I'll find Hoady and send him in. He can either fix the motor or tow you out."

That wasn't the solution Faith was hoping for. "Couldn't you tow me out?"

His expression told her just how distasteful he found that suggestion. "My boat's too big to handle that narrow channel you came through. There's another waterway I use, but it comes out on a completely different part of the lake. You'd be miles from your campground."

"Then could I call Hoady from your phone?"

"You could, if I had a phone."

Now she was desperate. She didn't want to spend her whole day waiting all alone for Hoady Fromme to rescue her. She had work to do, and besides, she didn't entirely trust the shifty-eyed little man.

"Let me come with you," she said. "You can dump me off at the first opportunity, wherever there's a road nearby or a house with a phone. I'll handle it from there."

He sighed, defeated. "Okay. But you're not getting in my boat like that." His eyes raked up and down her body, clearly disapproving of the mud still clinging to her.

"I don't suppose you'd let me use your shower."

"There's a hose in back of the house. Water's cold, but it's clean." Dismissing her, he turned.

"Wait a minute. Say that again."

He stopped and looked over his shoulder at her. "Say what?"

"About the hose."

"It's in back of the house. I said the water's cold but it's—"

"That's it! You're not even from this area, are you?" she declared triumphantly, pleased with her deduction but disappointed nonetheless. Jones Larabee wouldn't be part of her dissertation.

"Lady, what are you talking about?"

"The name's Faith. And I'm talking about the fact that you didn't grow up here."

The look in his eye was as close to sheer panic as she'd ever seen. "Where in the hell did you get an idea like that?"

"Your accent, your diction," she replied, her conviction unshakable. "A casual listener wouldn't pick it up, but I've made a study of the subtle nuances among the various dialects of Texas. It's a dying art, actually. In our mobile society, the dialects are blending more and more. But I'm intimately familiar with the Caddo Lake pronunciations. It's most notable in the way you say *water.*"

His eyes narrowed. "Think what you like." With that he continued toward the stairs, where he'd left his fishing gear, then headed for a small boat house to one side of the cabin.

I'm right, she thought. *And you're hiding from something, Mr. Jones Larabee.* What better place to hide than here in this private lagoon in the midst of an almost impenetrable swamp?

Faith figured if she didn't hurry he would leave without her. So she grabbed her tote bag and video camera case from the disabled dinghy and scampered around to the back of the house to douse herself with the hose.

As soon as Jones entered the boat house, safe for the moment from Faith Kimball's sharp blue eyes and even sharper ears, he consciously took three deep breaths until his heartbeat returned to normal. She'd almost scared him to death back there. He'd thought she'd actually recognized him.

It could happen. Dallas was a huge city, but he'd once been fairly visible, appearing in dozens of courtrooms in front of hundreds of jury members. Once, he'd even gotten his picture in the *Morning News* when he'd been the defense attorney in a high-profile bank fraud case.

But Faith hadn't recognized his face—only doubted his accent. Since moving here he'd deliberately cultivated a slower Southern drawl so he wouldn't stand out. His ef-

forts fooled most people. No one had ever questioned his
origins before. Only Faith.

She was a persistent little thing, he mused. And a beauty,
no doubt about that, with a round, angelic face framed by
a cloud of blond curls that spiraled halfway down her back.
Even the thin, still-healing scar on her forehead didn't de-
tract from her appeal. In fact, he hadn't noticed it at first,
so drawn was he to the intelligence behind those vivid sky
blue eyes and the implied promise of her cupid's bow of a
mouth.

The angry red scar on her slender thigh was a little harder
to ignore, but it was fresh yet. In time it would heal, just as
his had, until it was no more than a slight pucker in the
smooth, touchable skin. He imagined how it would feel—

Immediately he recognized the pang of sexual awareness, and guilt slapped his conscience. How could he even
think of another woman? Perhaps he didn't love Mary-
Lynn, not the way a prospective husband ought to, but he
was fond of her. She had been so loyal throughout his ordeal, hardly ever leaving his side. Although he couldn't be
with her and would never see her again, she didn't deserve
betrayal, even in his thoughts.

When the boathouse door opened and Faith reappeared, soaked to the skin but clean of the sticky swamp mud,
thoughts of Mary-Lynn were relegated to the back of his
mind. Damn, but a man would have to be dead and buried
not to respond to the way Faith's pale blue T-shirt clung to
every curve of her full, rounded breasts.

What a package she was—a body to tempt a saint, or in
his case a Good Samaritan, and a smile as innocent as that
of a kid on her first day at summer camp.

He had to get rid of her, and fast, before she beguiled
him any further.

With the balance of an experienced sailor she climbed onto his bass boat and stowed her tote bag and a mysterious-looking plastic case in the back. "Nice boat," she said as she cast off the line in back and pulled in the cylindrical bumper pad. "What are you fishing for today, crappie or bass?"

"I'll take either," he said. Hell, he wasn't even sure he could tell the difference. He'd only taken up fishing a month ago, when the weather had started to turn warm. He'd been itching for something to do and, spotting the cabin owner's fishing gear, had decided to give it a try.

His success was only marginal. He did, however, know that he could learn to love the sport. He had never experienced anything so relaxing as watching the beautiful arch of the lure sailing above the water, then slowly reeling it in as the boat swayed gently and the sun warmed his back. Actually getting a strike or catching a fish was only icing on the cake.

"Do you fish?" he asked casually, backing the boat out of its shelter and turning toward the channel.

"Mmm, yeah. Haven't gone in a while, though. Not since my dad died."

Funny how quickly priorities change sometimes, he thought. Initially he'd felt panicked by the idea of an outsider invading his space, asking questions. All he could think about was getting rid of her. But really, Faith wasn't such a threat. Even as his body responded to hers, his mind leapt at the prospect of a few minutes' feminine companionship. How long had it been since he'd carried on a conversation with any woman besides Hildy?

He would drive slowly to the marina, he decided. Even if they didn't exchange another word, he would enjoy

Faith's proximity. Just this once he would take a break
from his self-imposed isolation. It wouldn't do any harm,
so long as she didn't ask any more questions.

Two

Faith watched Jones, intensely fascinated with him. He might not be a native, but he was comfortable in his world.

He ignored the seat intended for the driver and stood before the steering wheel, keeping a keen eye ahead of the boat while navigating the narrow, snaking channel. Although not as torturous as the one through which Faith had reached Jones's island, this one was still tricky. Several times the boat shuddered when the motor kissed something underwater, causing Faith to hold her breath.

Jones hardly blinked.

As they passed a triangle formed by three huge cypress trees, a fish jumped out of the water, flashing silver in the dappled sunlight.

Jones shoved the throttle into neutral. "Did you see that?"

"Yes, I did. I hear there are some huge bass in this lake since they stocked it several years ago."

Jones stared at the spot where the fish had disappeared. Faith could see him battling with temptation. Finally he cut the engine and dropped anchor. "You don't mind if we stop for five or ten minutes, do you? I just want to cast a couple of times."

She nodded. "Okay with me." Faith liked the peaceful atmosphere of this sheltered spot. There was a certain primeval feel to this part of the bayou, as if no human had ever touched it.

"I brought an extra pole," he said. "You're welcome to throw out a line."

"Okay, thanks." She hadn't realized how much she'd wanted to fish until he'd invited her.

With a minimum of fuss Jones opened the tackle box, chose a purple worm lure, and started to cast. Faith found a yellow spinner for herself, attached it to the end of her line and moved to the opposite end of the boat.

Her father had taught her that fishing was a quiet sport. And since Jones didn't appear eager to chat, she kept her mouth closed, although there were hundreds of questions she wanted to ask him. She was particularly anxious to know why he was letting her fish with him at all. It seemed odd, given his initial animosity toward her.

As the minutes passed in silence, Faith's awareness of the man increased. She tried to concentrate on her casting, but how could she *not* notice that body of his when he ran around half-naked? He had a helluva tan for this early in the year, she thought, watching the bronzed muscles of his back bunch and stretch as he made a long, lazy cast.

He caught her staring at him. "Did I do something wrong?"

"What?" Self-consciously she started reeling in her forgotten lure, which was probably dragging the bottom by now.

"My casting. The way you were looking, I thought maybe my form was bad or something."

"There's nothing wrong with your form," she said, far more sincere than he would ever know.

They didn't speak again for a long time. The only sounds were the chatter of birds in the trees, the insects buzzing and the occasional whir, plop and click as she and Jones cast their lines. But Faith had the odd sensation that a bond was forming. Sharing a boat and a patch of sunlit water with a man was a curiously intimate experience.

The sun rose higher and the temperature climbed with it. Jones paused to take the green bandanna out of his pocket and mop his forehead. He then twisted the cloth into a rope and tied it around his head.

With that dark, shaggy hair and the tan, he could have been a savage, Faith mused. Mentally she replaced his threadbare cut-offs with a loincloth, then turned away so he wouldn't sense the heat in her face.

"You are the same man who rescued me," she said quietly, without looking at him again. "There couldn't be two of you."

He sighed. "If I admit that it was me, will you stop pestering me about it?"

She couldn't help but smile. She'd never met such a reluctant hero before. "If you'll let me say thank you. Thank you for saving my life."

"You're welcome," he said gruffly.

"You could have been killed yourself," she said. "It's not every man who will—"

He threw her a warning look.

"Right. 'Nough said. Have you caught a lot of fish in this spot before?" she asked. Despite the jumping fish they'd seen earlier, neither of them had gotten a strike all morning.

"No, not really. I'm still shopping for a really good spot."

"I don't think this is it," she said. "Not today, anyway. What do you say we pull anchor and try another place?"

He shrugged. "Fine by me. You pick out the next one."

It took her a long time to find a suitable spot. Finally, after exploring several inlets, she selected a shady area along the edge of one of the river roads.

"Why here?" Jones asked, although he didn't hesitate to drop the anchor.

"I don't know. My dad taught me to pick out a spot that feels right, and this one does."

With a shrug Jones switched to a frog lure, but Faith kept her yellow spinner. Within five minutes she had a fish on the end of her line. It was a big one, judging from the fight it gave her. A rush of adrenaline energized her as Jones stepped up behind her, silently urging her on. She played the fish just right, tiring it out until she could pull it out of the water without it jumping off the hook.

Jones stood waiting with the net. "That's a nice one," he said. "Must be at least two pounds."

"Oh, pound and a half, maybe," she said modestly as she removed the hook from its mouth. "A meal's worth, anyway. Where's the stringer?"

His face fell. "You aren't thinking of killing and eating him, are you?"

"Well, it's hardly trophy size."

He shook his head. "No, I mean, I don't usually keep them. I let them go."

"Oh, I see." So, her savage was squeamish. She never would have guessed. Then again, maybe she was being unfair. Perhaps he simply had a healthy respect for life—any life, be it a woman injured in a car accident or a dumb fish.

Mourning the loss of a tasty fried fillet, she eased the net out of his grip and dumped the contents back into the water. This was Jones's expedition, after all, so he got to call the shots. "Bye, fish," she said. "Luck's with you today."

Jones was standing close enough to her that she could feel the heat emanating from his body. He watched with a satisfied grin as the fish swam away. When he turned that grin on her, something inside her melted. She saw nothing of the meanness Hoady had warned her about.

As if suddenly remembering himself, Jones moved away from her, then busied himself riffling through the tackle box. "What kind of lure are you using, anyway?" he muttered.

"Try a spinner," she said, hiding a secret smile. She had the fleeting suspicion that Jones Larabee was warming up to her just a little. She wasn't sure why that mattered, but it did. Though she wouldn't be interviewing him for her dissertation, she wanted this puzzling man to like her.

They remained at that spot for an hour more, catching and releasing three more bass between them. But as the day's heat increased and their shade disappeared, the action petered out.

"I think the fish have gone somewhere cooler," Faith said.

Jones pulled in his line. "Yeah." He scanned the horizon, shielding his face from the sun with his hand. "I'll take you to the Sinclair Marina. You can call from there and make whatever arrangements you want."

Her heart sank. She could easily have spent all day fishing with Jones, and to hell with work on her dissertation.

She felt a small pang of guilt at her laziness. Before her accident, she had worked night and day on her paper with feverish enthusiasm. At the same time she'd been applying for teaching positions at institutions all over the Southwest, anticipating her Ph.D. in anthropology. She'd been burning the candle at both ends. That might be why she hadn't been alert enough to avoid the hit-and-run truck.

Since she had come so close to losing her life, however, she'd slowed down considerably. She already had more than enough material to support her theory, and her adviser had extended her dissertation deadline, so there was no hurry. What was wrong with spending a day fishing?

Jones had other plans for her, that's what was wrong, she thought, watching him neatly stow the lures in his tackle box and the poles in their niches on the side of the boat. He was ready to be rid of her, even if he *had* decided she wasn't such a horrible person after all.

"What's in there?" Jones asked, pointing to the plastic case Faith had stored in back of the boat.

"My videotape recorder," she replied as she slathered sunscreen on her face. "I was planning to film you—"

"Like hell!" he objected, scowling fiercely.

"Relax. I've never filmed anyone against their will." She rubbed sunscreen onto her legs, putting a little extra on her healing scar. Feeling the heat of his gaze on her, she became self-conscious about the scar and turned her back on him to rummage around in her tote bag. "Besides, since you're not from Caddo Lake, I'm not interested in making you a star."

He looked relieved. "Why's that?" he asked as he pulled up the anchor.

"Because I'm interviewing lifelong residents of the area for my doctoral dissertation, and you don't qualify."

"What are you studying?" He made no move to start the motor.

"I don't think you'd really be interested," she said, hedging. She'd learned long ago that no one outside her own esoteric field gave a flip about her work.

"Yes, I would. Tell me about it." He propped his lean hips against the back of the driver's chair and crossed his arms, waiting. Apparently they weren't going anywhere until she obliged.

"Well, if you insist, the subject matter is anthropology. Using the same protocol as Dr. Alfred Kermit, who studied the folklore and superstitions of this area thirty years ago, I'm trying to draw a negative correlation between economic growth and the survival of folkways and the specialized traditions peculiar to an isolated geographical location." That ought to stifle his curiosity.

He surprised her by nodding thoughtfully. "You're trying to prove that development and tourism are destroying the backwoods feeling that makes this place unique."

So, he understood. She wondered what kind of education he'd had. "That's about the size of it. Dr. Kermit's films are filled with barefoot men and women fishing for their living, smoking hand-carved pipes and strumming banjos, drinking homemade whiskey and telling the most outrageous stories.

"Most of it's gone, now," she said wistfully. "I've interviewed some of the children and grandchildren of those people. They still fish, but they also listen to rap music, watch movies on their VCRs and buy their clothes at Walmart just like everyone else. They remember some of the stories, but most have lost the art of *telling* a story."

Jones watched her, both amused and saddened by her passion for her work and the reality of what her research uncovered. He thought briefly of asking her if she'd met Miss Hildy, then decided not to. Although he imagined Faith would turn cartwheels at the prospect of interviewing an authentic medicine woman—a throwback to another time—he would have to ask Hildy first. He respected her privacy just as she respected his.

He turned the ignition key. "You hungry? They serve a pretty decent cheeseburger at the marina."

The shine of excitement returned to her eyes. "Starved. And it'll be my treat." When he started to object, she cut him off. "Consider it payment for being my fishing guide. I haven't enjoyed a morning like this in...well, in quite a few years." A shadow crossed her face, fleeting but definite.

"When did your father die?"

"Am I that transparent? He died last year. But he was sick for a long time before that."

"What was wrong with him?" Jones asked. He was exceeding the bounds of polite conversation, but suddenly he had to know.

She answered readily enough. "Lung cancer. Smoked like a chimney, right to the end."

Who could blame the man? Jones thought. When you're handed a death sentence, you might as well enjoy whatever pleasures remain in your life, right to the end. "What about your mother?"

"She lives in Florida. They divorced years ago, so she wasn't around when Dad died."

"You handled it alone, then?" God, how awful for her.

She nodded, then smiled unexpectedly. "It wasn't so bad, not all of it. We became a lot closer. I learned more about him during the year he lived with me than I had in the preceding twenty-six."

It wasn't so bad? He couldn't think of anything worse than watching someone you love die by slow, painful degrees.

"What about your folks?" Faith asked. "Are they still living?"

He should have expected it, he realized. For a while he'd let down his barriers and engaged Faith in normal, getting-to-know-you questions and answers. Now she was reciprocating. It was only natural.

So how did he answer her? Earlier, he would simply have told her to mind her own business. But that was before he knew she liked to fish and that she'd loved her father—and had gone through hell for him. That knowledge made it hard for Jones to be nasty to her.

"I don't have any family," he said offhandedly. "I'm, uh, an orphan." Why did he find it so hard to lie? He used to routinely twist the truth in a courtroom without an ounce of remorse. What was happening to him?

"Okay, I get the message," she said.

Obviously she didn't believe him. Not only was he a reluctant liar, he was a bad one. He felt as if he was cheating her, refusing to talk about himself after she'd opened up to him. But those were the breaks.

He pushed the throttle forward, and the boat surged ahead. He made sure they went fast enough that the engine noise would make further conversation impossible.

At the marina Jones ordered a cheeseburger and fries for Faith and a chef salad with whole-wheat Texas toast for himself, then paid for it with the ten-dollar bill Faith had obstinately stuffed into his hand. When he brought the tray to their outdoor table, she gave the salad a questioning look.

"I thought you wanted a cheeseburger," she said.

He shrugged. "When I was placing the order, suddenly a salad sounded better." It must be Hildy's influence, he decided. All that scolding about eating his greens was bound to have an effect on him.

Faith still thought his choice was odd. Most men she knew just didn't like salads. Certainly Jones didn't need to lose any weight. No, his body was about as lean and fit as any she'd seen. The more she observed him, the more puzzling he became.

His wallet, which he'd casually laid on the table, was a perfect example of his perplexing nature. It was made of eelskin, a finely crafted, expensive piece if she'd ever seen one. And it was monogrammed. A tiny gold plate bore the initials L. J. Not J. L.

Holy— The man was living under an assumed name, she realized with a jolt. What was he hiding from? Was he a fugitive from the law? Avoiding child support payments? A federal witness, relocated through the witness protection program? Or just a burned-out business executive who ran away?

At that point she should have shoved down that cheeseburger, thanked him for the fishing and gotten the hell out of there. He could be an ax murderer, for all she knew. But she sat right there, stretching every minute she was given with him. Her curiosity and fascination grew. So did her attraction.

"Who are you?" She didn't even realize she'd spoken the words aloud until his head snapped around.

The panicky look had returned to his hazel eyes, but it was quickly replaced by a coldness she didn't like at all. "We had a nice morning," he said evenly. "Don't ruin it."

They finished the meal in silence. When she was done, Faith murmured some inane pleasantry, grabbed her things and went inside to use the pay phone.

Forcing her mind to the problem at hand, Faith flipped through the pages of the slim local phone book until she found the number she wanted. After digging a quarter from her tote bag, she shoved it into the phone and punched in the number, her back turned resolutely toward the plate glass window that faced outside, where she'd left Jones.

"Black Cypress Campgrounds," Hoady Fromme answered in a bored voice.

Faith explained her predicament to him. He listened patiently until she mentioned just exactly where the dinghy was stranded.

"Missy, you're nuts if you think I'm going anywheres near Jones Larabee's place," he said. "I told you not to go there. I told you there'd be trouble. You broke the pull cord on the motor, now you can figure out how to get the boat back where it belongs. And don't be thinkin' you'll get your deposit back if the boat's not returned by tonight, either."

"But it's not my fault your equipment is faulty," she argued. "Why should you keep my seventy-five dollars?" That was money she could scarcely afford to spend. Her salary as a teaching assistant at the university was paltry at best, and the accident, though covered by insurance, had cost her quite a bit out of pocket.

"Because that's the way it works, that's why," Hoady said smugly. He hung up more forcefully than was necessary.

Frustrated, Faith considered her options. First, she would ask if this marina could rent her another boat. Next she would navigate back through the swamp, tie up the disabled dinghy behind her, and tow it to the campgrounds. Then she would have to return to the marina with the boat—and she would still be stranded.

Just thinking about all those logistics exhausted her. And when she saw the hourly rates for even the smallest motor boat, she was downright depressed.

As he waited at the window to pay for the gas he'd pumped, Jones overheard most of Faith's conversation with Hoady. Then he'd deliberately lingered, listening as she tried to negotiate with the marina for a boat. She wasn't having much luck.

He wondered why he cared. She'd certainly gotten under his skin in no time flat. Resolutely reminding himself that personal entanglements were not an option for him, he left the marina with only a couple of backward glances, intending to wipe pretty Faith Kimball and her dilemma out of his mind.

He set out toward the Big Lake section of Caddo, far from the swampy muck of the bayou, where he could swim without the fear of sharing his space with some vile swamp creature. He anchored the boat, then dived into the cold water and began to swim.

He'd once considered himself a pretty good swimmer, but it had been years since he'd been in a pool. Now he felt awkward in the water. Gradually, however, his splashy, choppy strokes evened out and he found his rhythm. The exertion felt great.

He swam circles around the boat until he was exhausted, then hoisted himself aboard and rested, letting the sun warm and dry him. And still he couldn't stop thinking about Faith—how her hair formed a glowing halo around her face, and the way her nose had started to turn pink from the sun, and most especially how she'd smeared that sunscreen lotion on her shapely legs.

But it wasn't just her looks that drew him. He liked her easy conversation, her passion for her work and the way she'd cheerfully let that big, fat fish swim away in deference to his softheartedness.

He couldn't stand to kill anything anymore—not even the spiders that constantly got into the cabin. Once, just as he was about to smash one of the creatures out of existence, he'd noticed the huge web it had built in the corner of his living room. After spending a good ten minutes contemplating the complexity and the sheer beauty of the fragile structure, he couldn't bring himself to destroy its creator. He had caught it in a cup and thrown it outside. He hadn't killed a spider since.

How could he have so much compassion for fish and spiders, then be so indifferent to Faith Kimball's plight?

It was a matter of survival, he answered himself. Faith, with her overabundance of curiosity, posed a threat to the path he'd chosen. He headed for home, more determined than ever to put their encounter behind him.

For the rest of the afternoon, as he puttered around the cabin, he kept an eye out the front window, wondering when she would return for her rented dinghy. Storm clouds were moving in. If she didn't get on with it, she'd be caught in the rain.

He fixed a microwave pizza for dinner, along with another salad made from Hildy's tasty produce. Still, there was no sign of Faith.

She had probably decided to wait until tomorrow. That meant seventy-five dollars would go into Hoady Fromme's pocket, money he hardly deserved.

What the hell. Jones could buzz over to the Black Cypress Campgrounds and be back before dark. It looked as if the rain would hold off. He wouldn't even have to see Faith Kimball if he didn't want to.

Problem was, he wanted to. Just once more.

Three

Faith allowed herself a huge yawn as she walked back to her campsite from the public showers. Although it wasn't yet dark, she felt like burrowing into her sleeping bag and hibernating until morning. That was the kind of day she'd had.

Her attempt to rent a boat from the Sinclair Marina had met with failure. Discouraged, she'd ended up hitching a ride back to her campgrounds, then again confronting Hoady. With her patience paper thin, she had threatened to sue him if he tried to keep her deposit. He had finally agreed to give her until tomorrow to return the disabled dinghy—*if* she would rent another boat from him and retrieve the first one. He was adamant about not going near Jones Larabee's island himself.

Jones Larabee. Or maybe it was Larabee Jones, depending on whether she believed his word or his monogram. Her encounter with the mysterious loner had been by far the most unsettling event of the whole day.

For a man who had shunned society to live alone in the swamp, he certainly seemed to have enjoyed her company—to a point. Was he a reluctant hermit as well as a reluctant hero? If so, what had driven him to seek a life of isolation? How did he live? Where did he get his money?

You idiot, she thought, berating herself as she reached the small, red dome tent that marked her campsite. Jones could easily be involved in something illegal. Maybe he grew marijuana back there in the swamp. And she was nuts for nursing this curiosity about him. She should just forget about him. Now that she had officially thanked him for saving her life, their business was finished.

Her stomach growled ominously as she unzipped the tent flap. She would cook dinner... but then a roll of distant thunder echoed her stomach's rumble, changing her mind. She could smell rain in the air. Building a fire to roast hot dogs was out of the question.

She would have to satisfy herself with cheese and crackers in her tent. That decision made, she went to her station wagon and retrieved a few snackables from the cooler. The clouds were moving in quickly, she noticed. The temperature had dropped several degrees in the past few minutes, and the wind had picked up.

She hoped she wasn't in for a bad storm. Although she knew her tent was sturdy and rainproof, she wouldn't be able to sleep through a night of loud, blustery thunderstorms. She grabbed her food and scrambled into the tent, then zipped it, making sure all flaps were securely tied down.

She had just changed into her nightshirt and was laying out her modest feast on a paper towel when she thought someone said her name. She tensed and listened, but all she heard was the howl of the strengthening wind.

"Is someone out there?" she called, her heart hammering inside her chest. Although there were other campers around, she felt suddenly vulnerable.

"Faith, it's Jones Larabee. I wanted to let you know I brought your boat back."

She broke a fingernail getting the flap unzipped. When she stuck her head out, she found herself looking at his jean-clad knee. At least he was dressed decently, she thought as her gaze traveled upward. But on second thought, he looked just as sexy clothed as he did half-naked. His faded jeans, soft from many washings, clung to his lean thighs and hips with loving familiarity, and his Texas Rangers T-shirt, cut off at the waist, revealed a tanned strip of rock-hard stomach muscles.

"Why?" The single word almost stuck in her dry mouth. "This morning you said it was too much trouble."

He knelt on one knee, bringing his face close to hers. "I overheard you talking to Hoady, and I didn't want that skunk keeping your deposit."

Jones's change of heart surprised her. But then, he'd made a habit of surprising her from the moment they'd met. "Thank you." She couldn't think of anything else to say.

"Hoady's lucky he already went home for the day, or I might have told him what I think of the way he treats his customers."

The thought made her smile wickedly. "You would have scared the poor man half to death." Hoady, who was already leery of Jones, would have dissolved into a pool of abject terror if he were actually subjected to another face-to-face meeting with his angry nemesis.

"It's no more than he deserves, sending a woman out alone into the swamp in that piece of junk he calls a boat. What if you'd gotten lost and the motor had quit in some isolated place where you couldn't get help? You might have been stuck for days."

"I had a paddle," she said, though his concern warmed her.

Lightning flashed, accompanied seconds later by a loud boom. Faith cringed and Jones winced. "Looks like I'd better be on my way," he said with a wary eye skyward. As he spoke, the first fat drops began to pelt down on them, hitting the tent's taut nylon with loud splats.

Now it was Faith's turn to be concerned. The clouds moving in from the southwest were thick and black as cast iron, blanketing the setting sun and bringing on an early dusk.

"You can't leave now," she objected. "Even if you don't get struck by lightning, you'll get soaked by the rain and you'll have to navigate in the dark." She shivered just thinking about how black that swamp would be.

"I can find my way in the dark," he said. Arguing with him, the sky released a renewed flurry of drops.

"But not when it's raining buckets," she insisted. Her hair was getting wet from the downpour. She pulled inside and opened the flap wider. "For heaven's sake, get in here before you're soaked through. You can at least wait out the worst of the storm."

He hesitated. Clearly he felt uncomfortable accepting her hospitality, humble though it was. Then another flash of lightning and a clap of thunder, louder than the last one, seemed to convince him. He dived into the shelter she offered, leaving his feet outside just long enough that he could take off his battered tennis shoes. The moment he zipped up the flap, a torrential rainfall began in earnest.

Big mistake, Faith thought as she tucked her sleeping bag securely around her bare legs. She should never have invited him in. Here in this confined space, Jones's blatant masculinity was overwhelming. His wide shoulders and long legs seemed to fill the tent, and the scent of him—the smell of damp hair and cotton and clean skin—wrapped its tendrils around her like one of the jungle vines she'd seen in the swamp. The enforced closeness between them was potently arousing and a little scary.

He pulled his long legs under him to sit Indian-style on her extra blanket, then took note of his surroundings. "I've interrupted your dinner, I see," he said, nodding toward her crackers and cheese.

"And quite a feast it is, too. Want some?"

"I've already eaten." He appeared antsy as he looked around for something to occupy his hands. Finally he picked up her portable radio. "Mind if I turn this on?"

"No, go ahead. Maybe we can get a weather report."

He fiddled with the dial until he found a station with a signal strong enough to be heard over the crackles of static. The news wasn't good. The line of thunderstorms moving through the area was substantial, expected to bring strong winds and possibly hail. The county was under a tornado watch.

Faith sighed. "I wish I hadn't heard that."

"Do storms bother you?" Jones asked.

She jumped a good two inches at the next deafening boom of thunder. "Does that answer your question? Really I'm no more frightened than the next person when I have a roof over my head. But when nothing separates me from the raging elements except a thin sheet of nylon, I tend to get . . . nervous."

She was more than nervous, Jones decided. Although it was growing dark enough that he couldn't see her well, he knew she was shivering—not only from the temperature drop, but with fear. He could almost smell it. He could definitely smell the electricity in the air, and not all of it came from the storm.

"We'll be okay," he said. "I'm glad you talked me into staying, though. It would have been a rough trip home."

The wind challenged his words, roaring around the tent, snapping the nylon and causing nearby trees to creak and groan. The rain fell with the force of a waterfall cascading over the tent.

By the time Faith finished her cheese and crackers, the darkness was thick. Yet Jones knew exactly where she was. Her case of nerves had grown into an almost tangible terror, which rolled off her in waves.

"Is it ever going to stop?" she demanded in a shaking voice.

Jones recognized the warning signs of a full-blown anxiety attack. Mary-Lynn had experienced them often enough, although it wasn't thunderstorms that had frightened her.

"It'll be okay," he soothed, reaching for her hand. When he found it, it was icy cold. He slowly moved closer until he sat next to her on her air mattress. His arm stole around her trembling shoulders.

Rather than object, as he thought she might, she snuggled closer to him, burrowing her head in the hollow of his shoulder. He held her close, warming her body with his until the shivering stopped.

In his head he knew she accepted simple comfort from him and no more. But his body disagreed. Although he was unable to see her, there were plenty of other physical signals for his senses to collect—the skin of her midriff, shielded only by her thin nightshirt, soft and warm against his palm; her silky hair tickling his face; and the sweet, womanly smell of her that seemed to permeate his very pores. Even her breathing turned him on.

"I feel ridiculous," she said into his chest. "I mean, I hardly even know you, and..."

"Shh," he said. No, she didn't know him, and she never would. He would make sure of that. He was so tempted to tell her everything and satisfy her curiosity, but he dared not. If he did, he might well end up in exactly the same kind of untenable situation that had forced him to leave his hometown, his friends, his family, his fiancée.

"I think it's letting up, isn't it?" Faith asked hopefully.

Jones didn't have the heart to answer her. If anything, the storm had intensified. Between the almost constant claps of thunder, car doors slammed and engines started, evidence that many of their fellow campers had opted for higher ground.

A weather bulletin on the radio informed them that funnel clouds had been sighted in Marshall and Kildare, both within twenty miles of Caddo Lake. The tornado watch was upgraded to a warning.

"I don't want to alarm you, but I think we should get out of here," Jones said.

"And go where?" The panic had edged back into her voice as she pulled away from him.

"The shower building," he replied, picturing a sturdy brick structure. "Isn't there one just up the road?"

"Yes. Good, that's a good idea. Just let me put some clothes on..." She sounded calmer, now that she had something to occupy her.

Jones waited in the darkness as she slipped on a pair of jeans under her nightshirt just inches from him, driving his imagination wild. He guessed that ordinarily she wouldn't have been so uninhibited, but speed was of the essence.

"You drive," Faith said, handing him the keys.

When they both had their shoes on, they made a dash for the car, but they might as well have saved the effort. Their clothes were soaked to the skin. Jones turned on the heater, flipped the windshield wipers to high speed, then crept cautiously onto the narrow road that meandered through the small campgrounds. One wrong turn, he thought, and they could end up fender-deep in swamp muck.

Somehow, though he couldn't see an inch in front of the car, he made it to the main road and then the public shower building without mishap. He parked close to the door. Then he and Faith made a break for shelter.

"Whew!" Faith exclaimed, visibly relaxing now that she had a roof over her head. "I never thought I'd be so happy to see this nasty building. I feel much safer."

Jones wasn't so sure they were safe. The small building had only a corrugated fiberglass roof, which a high wind could easily whip away. He was also bothered by the fact that no one else had taken shelter here. He tried not to reveal his uneasiness, however. Unless he wanted Faith's anxiety to return, he needed to make her believe he had everything completely under control.

At least the place had lights.

Faith sat down on the wooden bench between the doors leading to the men's and women's sides of the building, leaned her head against the brick wall and closed her eyes.

Jones took the opportunity to study her. She looked like a half-drowned cat, with her hair plastered to her head and her clothes dripping wet, and yet she managed to maintain an air of fragile beauty. His gaze was drawn to her pink nightshirt. The wet, nearly transparent fabric clung to the bare skin beneath it, revealing firm, rounded breasts with nipples that pebbled against the cool night air.

He tore his gaze away and sat down next to her, close but not touching. His libido had taken enough of a beating for one night. "You okay now?" he asked.

"Yes, I feel much better." She opened her eyes and fixed him with her clear blue gaze. "I'm sorry I was such a baby."

"It was understandable."

"You're not living up to your reputation, you know. Offering comfort, that is. The folks around here are scared to death of you. Hoady says you tried to kill him."

"That's a gross exaggeration."

"Then what really happened?"

That damn curiosity of hers was going to lead to trouble, Jones thought. But he didn't see any harm in telling her this particular story. "He was setting trotlines in my lagoon. I didn't want to have to deal with him coming around every day to check them, and I didn't want to look at those ugly floats all the time. I told him to take his lines elsewhere. And when he ignored me, I got out a shotgun and—"

Faith gasped. "You didn't!"

"I shot into the air." Jones laughed. "I didn't think fat little Hoady could move so fast."

Faith shared his laughter for a moment, but then she sobered. "Hoady's not the only one. The man at Jasper's Grocery, Bill Something, I think his name was, thinks you're a fugitive from the law, probably a murderer. He says he saw your picture in a post office."

Bill Holt. Jones never had liked the man, or his nosy questions. "Bill can think what he likes."

"It seems everyone has a different opinion as to what you're doing all alone in the swamp, but everyone agrees about one thing. They all say you're meaner than a snake, and they advised me to keep my distance."

"But you didn't."

"Because I knew you weren't mean. I remembered how you talked to me after the accident, how you coaxed me to unbuckle my seat belt. And I remembered how kind you were when you wiped the blood off my face and bandaged my leg."

Now they were in uncomfortable territory. Jones shrugged. "Yeah, well, you needed help and I happened to be there."

"But you're not mean," she insisted. "Why do you let everyone believe you are?"

"So they'll keep their distance. Of course, that doesn't deter *some* people." He gave her a pointed look.

"Why do you want them to keep their distance?"

"Faith, will you stop with the questions?" He did his best to bark at her, but it came out sounding like a plea instead. "I can't answer them."

"Is it something illegal?"

"No, dammit." Not unless disappearing was a felony. It was if you did it to get out of paying your debts, but he didn't fall into that category. Practicing law had netted him more money than he knew what to do with.

"Then why won't you tell me?"

"Why do you need to know?" he shot back.

"Because..." She took a deep breath, then placed her hand over his where it rested on his knee. "Because I like you, and I want to know you better."

Her message was unmistakable. For him to respond to it was unthinkable. He jumped up from the bench as if he'd been scalded and took two long strides away from her. Even if he could allow someone to get close to him—which he couldn't—there was Mary-Lynn.

He read the hurt plainly in Faith's eyes and felt like an absolute heel. This was all his fault. Maybe she'd been the one to seek him out, but he had allowed her to pull him from his shell. He had let her get too close.

"It's nothing personal, Faith," he said.

"Well, it *feels* personal."

"It's not—please believe me. You're an attractive, interesting woman, and under normal circumstances, I would jump at the chance to know you better." A lot better. "But I can't. I'm . . . committed elsewhere."

"Girlfriend?"

"Fiancée."

"Who is she?"

"Her name's Mary-Lynn."

"What's her last name?" Faith asked with a skeptical tilt to her head.

"Hoffman," he blurted out because he wanted to convince her he wasn't making this up. Immediately he regretted his impulsive admission. There was little chance Faith could or would locate Mary-Lynn, even given her last name. After all, she didn't know where he was from. But it worried him anyway.

"When are you getting married?"

"We're not, I guess."

"Then she's not your fiancée."

"She still has my ring." Maybe. He'd left her a note, telling her to sell the ring and find someone new, but he doubted she'd done it. Mary-Lynn was a sentimental soul.

"Then why—"

"Faith!" He was getting truly angry now. Her curiosity was understandable, but she was invading his privacy. "No more questions." In a quieter tone he added, "Listen, the rain is letting up. I'm going to turn on the car radio and see if I can get an updated weather report."

She watched him walk away, feeling utterly wretched. She'd made a fool of herself. Even if Jones were attracted to her, he wouldn't give in to temptation. His loyalty to the mysterious Mary-Lynn Hoffman made him that much more appealing.

She stepped into the ladies' room to have a look at her hair. What she saw made her groan. Jones *wasn't* attracted to her. How could he be? She looked about as appealing as a wet log.

She pulled a comb out of her purse and tried to make sense of her damp, curly mane.

What had happened to Mary-Lynn? Faith found herself wondering. Had the woman jilted him? Had she died?

Damn, she had to stop this endless speculation about Jones Larabee's life. He didn't welcome her curiosity, and he had a right to his privacy—much as that irked her.

"Faith?" His voice through the bathroom door sounded a bit anxious.

"Be out in a minute," she called back. She gave herself one final appraisal in the streaked mirror, making sure she carried a confident expression. It wouldn't do to let him know how thoroughly humiliated she was. She would give the impression that his rejection had made barely a ripple in her psyche.

When she emerged, he was pacing the concrete floor, his thumbs hooked in his jeans pockets. "There you are."

Had he suspected her of being so distraught that she'd thrown herself in the lake and drowned? "Here I am, all right."

"The weather bureau has given the all-clear. Seems the worst of the storm has moved on into Louisiana and Arkansas."

"That's good to know. Let's get out of here." She was anxious to send Jones home, dark or no dark. Maybe then things could get back to normal.

But *normal* simply wasn't to be. As she turned her station wagon onto the narrow road that led to her campsite, Faith spotted flashing red and blue lights ahead of her and a general state of chaos that hadn't existed when they'd left.

Most of the other campers had apparently abandoned the area. Only three trailers remained. Of those, one had been ripped open like an aluminum can, with a gaping slash from stem to stern. Another trailer lay on its side. A deputy sheriff was examining the damage and trying to calm the distraught owners of the ripped-up camper.

An uprooted tree barred the station wagon's progress, as it had the sheriff's car. Faith cut the motor and got out, and Jones followed suit. As they drew nearer on foot, she could see great divets dug out of the treetops, as if a giant spoon had scooped away branches like so much soft ice cream.

Nothing but a direct hit by a tornado could have caused this much damage.

The deputy shone a flashlight in their faces as they approached. "You folks the owners?" he asked, nodding toward the trailer on its side.

"No," Faith answered, looking around anxiously, trying to get her bearings. "I had a tent. A red tent. It must be around here somewhere."

"Could that be it?" the deputy asked, shining his flashlight upward. Faith's gaze followed the beam of light until it reflected off a scrap of red nylon. Her tent was caught in the top of a tree, fifty feet up.

The implications made her dizzy. "Oh, my," she murmured as she leaned against the trailer.

"Oh, hell," Jones added, shaking his head. "That's a tough break."

"I'd say we're pretty lucky," Faith countered. "That's the second time you've saved my life, Jones. If you hadn't gotten me out of that tent, I would have sat there paralyzed with fear, and the tornado would have blown us both up into the tree right along with my tent!''

The deputy, whose attention had wandered back to the elderly couple snuffling over their loss, turned sharply as Faith made this speech. ''Jones?'' he said, shining the flashlight once more in Jones's face. ''Jones Larabee? What are you doing prowling around this time of night?''

Faith watched in amazement as Jones's expression transformed in a heartbeat from tender to surly. He looked just as he had that morning—was it only that morning?—when she'd first confronted him with the green bandanna.

''Yeah, it's me,'' he drawled. His imitation of the local dialect was nearly flawless. He didn't answer the deputy's question.

''You just watch your step,'' the deputy growled. ''There'll be no looting while I'm around.''

Jones groaned quietly. Faith could tell he was biting his tongue to keep from verbally tearing the idiot deputy's head off. Looting! Where did he get such nonsense?

''I'm going to check my boat—if I still have a boat,'' Jones said, turning sharply on his heel.

The deputy fixed his beady stare on Faith. ''Young lady, you know that man?''

''I certainly do. What of it?'' she asked belligerently. What did she have to lose? If he hauled her off to jail, at least she would have a roof over her head.

''I can tell you're not from around here. Jones Larabee's not a man to trifle with. You let down your guard, and you might just find your throat slit.''

''That is the most ridiculous thing I've ever heard,'' she retorted, her voice escalating in volume along with her temper. ''Jones has saved my life, not once but twice. Do you think he'd go to that much trouble just so he could kill me?''

The deputy winced with every word. "Would you lower your voice, please?"

"Why? Why not let *everyone* hear you slander a good man's name?"

Just then a hand that felt like steel clasped around her wrist. A voice every bit as harsh said to the deputy, "Would you excuse us, please?" and Jones dragged Faith several feet away.

"What's your problem?" she demanded, her dander still up from dealing with the deputy's unfounded accusations.

"I appreciate your confidence in me, Faith, but I don't need you defending me to some redneck lawman."

"Why not? He was slandering you! I'll warrant he doesn't have one shred of evidence to support his claim that you're some sort of deviant bent on violence."

"Just my reputation. Give me your keys."

"Why?" she asked, even as she handed them over.

"So I can park your car where it won't be in the way. Then I'm taking you home."

"But you *can't* let people say things like that about you. He said you might slit my throat."

Jones smiled evilly. "Did he, now?" On that note he turned and walked away.

Apparently Jones meant what he said. He enjoyed his unsavory reputation. He didn't want anyone cleaning it up for him. No sooner had she absorbed that fact than she realized what he'd just said to her. He'd said he was taking her home.

He meant *his* home. To spend the night.

Four

If her last trip through the swamp to Jones's island was unnerving, this one was terrifying, not to mention freezing. Faith huddled at Jones's feet on the floor of the bass boat, using the steering console as a windscreen, but it didn't do much good. As the boat bumped across open water, the wind whipped at her hair and her damp clothes until her teeth chattered.

They turned onto a narrow boat road, and Faith was relieved that Jones had to slow down. But her relief didn't last long. The dark, forbidding channel, which had seemed so pleasant the last time she'd passed through on a sun-dappled fishing expedition, now pulsed with menace. She could see and hear the fearsome night creatures that oozed through the water or hung from branches or rustled their feathers mysteriously while staring with malevolent yellow eyes.

Well, okay, she couldn't see any eyes, but she knew they were there all the same.

Jones idled the boat and looked down at her. "You okay?"

She couldn't actually see him, either, but she sensed his intense gaze. "F-fine," she said. She'd been enough of a 'fraidy-cat for one night. He would have to torture her with red-hot irons before she would admit that a few cypress trees and a little Spanish moss frightened her.

He leaned down and touched her arm. "You're freezing. Why didn't you tell me?"

"Because there's nothing you can do about it." Unless, since he seemed immune to the chill night air, he wanted to wrap his warm-blooded body around her shivering one. That obviously wasn't a possibility. "Let's just get where we're going, please."

"Wait a minute." He turned and lifted one of the padded bench seats, revealing a storage compartment underneath. After rummaging around among life vests and odd lengths of rope, he came up with a Windbreaker of some sort. "Try that. We're still a good fifteen minutes from the island."

Grateful for any respite from the wind, she murmured her thanks and shoved her arms through the sleeves of the jacket, which was far too large for her. Five seconds later she was screeching and trying to tear the garment off her body as fast as she could.

Jones whirled and stared at her. "What the hell?"

Her frenzied gyrations caused her to trip backward over a gas can and fall on her behind—for the second time today—but she managed to strip the Windbreaker off and fling it across the boat.

Jones blinded her with the boat's spotlight. "Mind telling me what you're doing?"

"There was something crawling around in that jacket besides me," she explained as sensibly as she could. She regained her feet and backed to the rear of the boat, as far from the offending Windbreaker as possible.

He refocused the spotlight on the jacket. With a skeptical expression he picked it up and shook it. To Faith's relief, something long and black fell to the deck with a thunk. She never thought she'd be grateful to see a snake, but at least she hadn't imagined the slithery thing she'd felt in one sleeve.

With little concern, Jones picked up the snake and tossed it overboard. "Don't worry, it's just a harmless water snake," he said. "They get into everything." Then he shook the Windbreaker again and examined it thoroughly before handing it to her. "Sorry. I should have checked it before for critters."

She took it reluctantly, loath to put it on again. Besides, all that adrenaline had warmed her up quite a bit. She laid the jacket aside. "I'm not so cold anymore," she said with a shaky chuckle.

He joined her, his laughter warm and rich. It was the first time she'd heard him laugh, she realized. "Poor Faith," he said, shaking his head. "Between me and Hoady and the tornado, and now a snake, you've had a pretty rotten day."

She nodded. He probably didn't realize that the worst part of her day had been when he'd rejected her. Jones was the first man to interest her in *that* way for a long time. Dating had been out of the question while her father had been ill. And after his death, she had thrown herself into her work as if the devil was chasing her, exhibiting every known Type A behavior pattern. But she was sure that, even when she was at the height of her workaholism, if a man like Jones Larabee had come along, she would have noticed.

And he was spoken for, dammit, by the mysterious Mary-Lynn Hoffman, the fiancée he wasn't planning to marry. Faith was determined to get to the bottom of this mystery.

"Come sit up here," he said, patting the driver's chair.

She obliged him, simply because she was still shaking from fear and cold, and she longed to sit close to his big, reassuring body.

After returning the spotlight to its brackets and adjusting it so that it shone on the black waters ahead of them, he swiveled her chair to the side and stood beside it. With the boat in gear he resumed navigating along the tortuous channel.

Faith was still acutely aware of the noises from the banks—the flapping and croaking and hooting of unidentified creatures—but now they didn't bother her as much. It was only as she and Jones were about to pull into the boathouse that she realized she'd been holding his hand.

She let go quickly—like maybe he wouldn't notice? *Sure, Faith.* If he didn't already think she was a fainthearted wimpette, he did now.

She was glad that he made no comment. She helped him secure the boat for the night, and then he led her wordlessly along a graveled path to the front stairs.

Jones's house was as charming inside as out, with rough-hewn log walls, comfortable-looking Early American furniture and a big stone fireplace. Although in Texas fireplaces weren't entirely necessary, Faith had always liked the ambiance of a warm, flickering blaze on a cool night.

Jones showed her around quickly. There was a small but serviceable kitchen replete with baskets and copper accents; a den with an overflowing bookshelf, some weightlifting equipment and several jigsaw puzzles; and a loft bedroom under the vaulted ceiling, which he pointed out from below. Although the cabin bore the unmistakable signs of sole male occupancy, like tennis shoes left on the rag rug in the living room and a few dishes stacked in the sink, it was an altogether inviting, cozy atmosphere. Faith immediately felt at home.

"Why don't you get out of those wet clothes?" Jones asked. "You can take a hot shower, if you want. I'll try to find you something to wear."

If any other man had made such a suggestion, she might have read something into it. But not Jones. His motives appeared to be perfectly pure...unfortunately.

"I'd like that," she said through her chattering teeth. Although the temperature probably was only in the fifties outside, and much higher inside, she couldn't seem to shake the shivers. She retreated to the bathroom, peeled out of her wet things, and took refuge under a steamy spray. She didn't even worry when she heard the bathroom door open. Through the wavy glass of the shower door, she saw a tanned arm extend inside, deposit a wad of clothing by the sink, then retreat.

Jones was disgusted with himself. What insanity had made him drag Faith here to spend the night? If he hadn't been so softhearted, wanting to return her dinghy, he wouldn't be in this mess. Then again, if he hadn't shown up at the Black Cypress Campgrounds, Faith might have ended up along with her tent in the top of a tree.

Still, after the tornado he could have seen her safely to some other shelter and left it at that. Now he was stuck with a houseguest who tempted him to the very brink of his self-control. In the boat, when she had clutched his hand with childlike trust, he'd felt an overwhelming urge to fold her into his arms and reassure her that everything would be okay. And then he would have kissed her, long and hard.

He wasn't much better off now. He tried to distract himself by making some of the herbal tea Miss Hildy had given him, but his thoughts were on the sleek body that was at this moment occupying his shower. He hadn't peeked when he'd opened the door to leave her a flannel shirt and a pair of sweatpants—but he'd wanted to.

By the time she emerged from his bathroom, he had loaded the dishwasher, wiped down the counter and set out a loaf of homemade honey bread—another of Hildy's offerings—on the cherry wood kitchen table. He had also kindled a small fire. Although the season for fires was long past, it was shaping up to be an unusually chilly night for April.

"Oh," she said when she saw the table setting. "You didn't have to go to this trouble."

"No trouble," he replied absently, his attention focused on how sexy she looked wearing his clothes. The red plaid shirt almost swallowed her whole, with the hem hitting her mid-thigh and the sleeves rolled up several times. Somehow, though, she managed not to look shapeless. The soft flannel outlined the curve of her full breasts in a way that made his mouth go dry.

He busied himself pouring tea.

"Mmm, thanks." She took a sip and almost choked. "Good Lord, what's in this stuff?" she asked when she'd stopped coughing.

"It's just an herbal tea," he said. Although Hildy's tea had an unusual flavor, it had never occurred to him that someone else might not like it. He drank gallons of the stuff.

"What kind of herbs?" she asked, pushing a stray blond curl out of her face and staring suspiciously into the cup.

"I'm not sure. Marigolds and periwinkles, something like that. Oh, and something called poke root. A friend gave it to me. I swear, I crave the stuff." He craved Faith Kimball even more. He wanted to bury his fingers in the mass of curls piled haphazardly atop her head.

"You have a friend?" she teased.

"Not everyone thinks I'm the devil's spawn. Give it here," he said, taking her cup and dumping it in the sink. "I have some regular tea around somewhere." He quickly located the tea bags, placed one in Faith's cup and covered it with boiling water from the kettle.

She nodded her thanks as he set it on the table in front of her. "So," she said as she stirred in a spoonful of sugar, "how long have you lived here?"

He straddled a chair across from her. "A few months."

"Hmm, I would have thought longer. This place has a real nice, lived-in feel."

"It *was* lived in—but not by me. Most everything you see was here when I moved in. I'm just renting the place un-til—" He stopped, appalled at what he'd almost blurted out. Faith had a way of knocking down barriers until he was as unprotected as a turtle without its shell. He'd better stay more alert.

"Until what?" she prompted.

"Never mind. You aren't going to interrogate me again, are you? If so, I'll send you packing. You can swim back to the Black Cypress." It was an empty threat and she knew it, although she looked hurt just the same.

She said nothing for a long time as she concentrated on buttering a piece of the honey bread. "Am I allowed to ask about this friend who bakes wonderful bread?"

"No. That is, she wouldn't want me to talk about her. She's a very private person."

"I see."

Jones felt like first-class pond scum. He wished he could make Faith understand that he had no choice in the matter. His personal life was off-limits.

When the silence had grown uncomfortable, he said, "You can sleep in my bed."

Her head jerked up and she stared at him, her sky blue eyes huge with surprise, or maybe alarm.

"I'll sleep on the couch," he quickly added, feeling guilty for having deliberately provoked her. He wondered what her reaction would have been if he hadn't amended the offer. She didn't seem the type to jump into bed with any man, even if she had already admitted an interest in him.

Of course, such speculation was pointless. Even if she came right out and offered, he wouldn't go to bed with Faith Kimball or any woman, ever again.

God, what a depressing realization.

Faith yawned elaborately. "It's been a long day. I think I'll turn in. But I hate putting you out of your own bed." She paused just long enough before saying, "I don't mind sleeping on the couch." She looked up at him with complete innocence.

Two can play at this game, he thought grimly as his body responded to her words against his will. It was no more than he deserved. "Take my bed," he said, playing it straight. "I sleep on the couch all the time. It's perfectly comfortable."

She nodded in acquiescence, thanked him for his hospitality, took her plate and cup to the sink and gracefully disappeared. The last he saw of her were her dainty bare feet retreating up the steep stairs to the loft.

He should have given her some socks. But he wasn't about to follow her into his bedroom and offer her a pair. Ensuring warm feet wasn't worth the risk of having her, him, and a bed all in the same proximity.

* * *

Although she was exhausted, Faith had a hard time falling asleep. For one thing, the bed smelled faintly of sunshine and soap and healthy male—like *him*. But the real problem was in her own mind, where questions without answers chased themselves like swallows darting in and out of a barn.

Who the hell was Jones Larabee, and why was he hiding out in the swamp? She had ruled out a criminal background. If he were some escaped convict, she reasoned, he would simply lie about his past to satisfy her and shut her up. Equally unbelievable was the idea that he could be avoiding alimony payments or child support.

Running from the IRS? Now that had possibilities, but only if his reasons for evading taxes were idealistic. Maybe he was a passionate member of one of those groups of people who truly believe income tax is unconstitutional.

Nah, that was pretty unlikely. He was too practical for that.

Chances were Jones Larabee was just someone who didn't want to be found. He might have suffered a mental breakdown and, unable to cope with his life, he'd simply dropped out. If such were the case, he wasn't nearly as stable and grounded as he seemed.

Face it, she told herself firmly. He wasn't the kind of guy she wanted to develop a lasting relationship with, not even a friendship. Whatever his deep, dark secret, it was likely to be unpleasant. So tomorrow, first thing, she would impose on him once more to ferry her to civilization. She would thank him for his kindness and then get the hell away from him.

With that matter firmly settled, she proceeded to spend the night tossing and turning and dreaming things she didn't dare think about on a conscious level.

By six-thirty the next morning she was wide awake. Deciding it was pointless to remain in bed, she got up and tiptoed downstairs. She shivered and rubbed her upper arms. It was freezing down here, at least five degrees colder than in the loft.

A nice, hot cup of coffee was what she needed. Last night she had seen a pot in the kitchen; presumably there was some coffee to go with it, and she intended to brew some.

As she passed through the living room, she couldn't help but notice her host in an uncomfortable-looking sprawl on the too-short sofa. The afghan he had used as a blanket was bunched up around his waist, leaving most of his long, muscular body exposed to the chilly morning air. He looked as though he felt the cold, too, with his arms crossed over his chest and his wide shoulders hunched.

She thought about covering him up, then decided that might be too personal and quite embarrassing if he should wake up. Instead she stoked the fire, which had died to embers.

After she'd kindled a lively blaze, she passed by the couch a second time and took a good long look, sucking in her breath. Jones was modestly clothed in boxer shorts, so it wasn't as if she were seeing anything she hadn't seen before. But, damn, he was one well-formed hunk of man.

She scooted on past, out of temptation's way. Halfway to the kitchen she skidded to a stop. Harvard Law School. *Harvard Law School?* Had those words really been emblazoned all over Jones's shorts?

So, Jones Larabee was probably a lawyer, she thought as she rummaged around in his cabinets for coffee and filters. That was almost as hard to believe as the possibility of his being a criminal. He didn't fit into the mold of the attorneys she had known, with their starched shirts and razor-cut hair and superior attitudes.

Maybe he was a prosecutor who'd sent a murderer to jail, she mused as she filled the glass pot at the sink, only the murderer had escaped and was trying to kill Jones, and that was why he was hiding out. Hmm, the scenario was appealingly romantic—and even more farfetched than her ax murderer theory. But perhaps some other sticky legal entanglement had sent him into hiding. A brush with organized crime, or even an ugly divorce case, could lead to life-threatening circumstances.

It disturbed her to think that someone might actually be trying to kill him.

As the coffee brewed she took a leisurely stroll around the cabin, more observant this time than she'd been last night. She wasn't invading his privacy, she reasoned. He had shown her everything already. She didn't plan to go poking around in drawers or peeking under the furniture.

She went first to the den. Outside the big picture window dawn was breaking, so that the titles on the bookshelves were barely readable without turning on a light. Mostly they were children's books: Nancy Drew and Hardy Boys mysteries, and classics like *Tom Sawyer, The Call of the Wild* and *Lord Jim.* These weren't Jones's books, then.

Some recent magazines were scattered over a coffee table—a fishing journal, crossword puzzles, a couple of general news magazines. There was also a newspaper from nearby Jefferson. Apparently he hadn't totally lost interest in the outside world.

A boom box sat in one corner with several cassette tapes scattered around: Mozart, Haydn, Tchaikovsky.

Nothing else she saw in the room told any secrets. She started to leave, figuring the coffee was about ready, when she noticed a closet door hanging ajar. *No,* she scolded herself. She wouldn't look inside. Resolutely she crossed the room, intending to shut the door on temptation. But the door wouldn't close.

Reflexively she opened it wider to see what was stopping it. Inside the closet was a stack of hunting and fishing trophies—deer heads, mounted fish, a stuffed pheasant and an otter posed unnaturally on a piece of driftwood. She quickly moved one of the deer heads out of the way and shut the door, noticing one other thing just before it slammed: a high school letter jacket, hung on a hook, that said Holland High on the sleeve.

"Did you find everything you were looking for?" a hard voice behind her demanded.

Her heart in her throat, Faith whirled around, a dozen denials on the tip of her tongue. But she knew what it looked like. He'd pretty much caught her red-handed, and she couldn't make excuses with those hard hazel eyes staring her down.

"Your closet door wouldn't close," she said, meeting his gaze as defiantly as she dared. All six-foot-plus of him, wearing nothing more than a pair of faded jeans only half fastened, loomed very close to her. For the first time, she saw what had frightened Hoady and some of the other locals. Jones was a man who didn't like to be crossed, and he was quick to let you know it.

There was nothing left for her to do except confess everything. "I came in here to look at your books. I didn't touch anything except the closet door, and that was only because it wouldn't shut and I hate closet doors that don't shut. And what do you care if I saw a bunch of old hunting trophies?"

He said nothing, but some of the fierceness left him. He relaxed his stance slightly, and his fists unclenched.

Encouraged, she continued, "I already knew you had a soft spot for animals. It's no surprise that you don't want to look at stuffed dead animals every time you walk in here. But I've learned nothing else about you except that you like crossword puzzles and classical music. And if you weren't so damn secretive, maybe I wouldn't be so damn nosy!"

"At least you admit it," he said as something akin to amusement crossed his features. But his scowl quickly returned.

"I'm an anthropologist," she said, folding her arms defensively. "We're a nosy lot."

He took a step back, then gestured for her to walk ahead of him to the kitchen. He was going to keep an eye on her from now on, she imagined. She really couldn't blame him.

He poured them both some coffee. "What do you want for breakfast?" he asked easily, putting their unpleasant encounter behind him.

She was too hungry to pretend otherwise. "I'll eat whatever you have. But why don't you let me fix it?" she asked. She figured his hospitality was wearing thin.

He rubbed absently at the back of his head, making her wonder if he had a headache. More likely it was a stiff neck from sleeping on that sofa. "Yeah, okay," he agreed. "There's ham and eggs in the fridge, bread in the bread box and corn flakes and pancake mix in the cabinet to the right of the stove. Whatever you decide to make, just make me some of the same. I'll be back in a few minutes."

He was frowning as he walked away, seemingly preoccupied with something. A few moments later she heard the shower running.

Since she was ravenous, Faith fixed scrambled eggs, ham and toast. She was just putting two steaming plates on the kitchen table when Jones reappeared, freshly showered and shaven, carrying the scent of soap and menthol shaving cream. At least he was wearing a shirt now, Faith noticed.

Jones's bare chest was a distraction she was finding harder and harder to ignore.

He sat down without a word and began to eat, but after a few bites he laid down his fork and stared out into space, his brow furrowed as if something heavy was on his mind.

"Is something wrong with the eggs?" she asked.

"Hmm? Oh, no, they're fine. I'm just not very hungry, I guess. Listen, as soon as you're done, I have to take you back to the campgrounds."

She nodded as her heart sank. She'd been hoping that maybe he was pondering whether he should open up to her. But whatever he was thinking about, it had nothing to do with her.

She quickly polished off her breakfast. If he wanted to be rid of her, there was no sense procrastinating. She stood and began clearing the table.

"Leave the dishes," Jones said. "We need to get going."

"Okay," she said with false brightness. "Just let me change back into my clothes, and I'll be ready."

She was relieved to find that her jeans and nightshirt, which she'd hung over a towel rack in the bathroom, were dry. She quickly wiggled into them, wishing desperately for a bra. Last night in the dark she hadn't thought too much about it, but now she did. She wasn't one of those small-breasted girls who could go without support and still feel comfortable.

When she had her shoes and socks on, she marched resolutely to the front door, where Jones waited for her, looking antsy. He handed her an old jacket, which she was happy to have for the sake of modesty as well as warmth.

As they stepped out on the front porch, she saw something that surprised her. A rather large woman, wearing overalls and a straw hat, was pushing a much-patched and

-painted canoe onto shore. Either she was ignorant of Jones's dastardly reputation...or she was his unnamed friend, the one who made herbal tea and baked bread.

"Oh, no," Jones groaned when he saw the woman. "Of all the...why now?"

Five

Jones couldn't find it in himself to be short with Miss Hildy, not even when his head felt as if someone had put an ax through it while he was sleeping, but she'd picked a damned inconvenient time to show up.

"Mornin', Miss Hildy," he said resignedly as he helped her with the single shopping bag she'd brought. "Weren't you here just yesterday?"

"I was, in fact," she said merrily. She glanced up at the porch, where Faith stood and watched with bright, curious eyes. "I see the little gal found you." Unmistakable innuendo colored Hildy's voice.

"It's not what you think," Jones grumbled. "As a matter of fact, we were just leaving."

"I won't keep you, then," Hildy said, though she continued on an unerring course toward the cabin. "But I just had to bring you some honey—I forgot it yesterday."

"Honey. Yes, I couldn't get along another day without that," he said dryly. He suspected that the real truth was that Hildy had somehow gotten wind of his overnight guest and couldn't resist coming over for a peek. She sometimes stopped in at the Blue Ribbon Café to sell the owner her baked goods; she'd probably overheard that obnoxious deputy carrying on about how Jones Larabee had seduced an innocent camper who was down on her luck.

"Well, you're in a mood," Hildy said as she laboriously climbed the stairs. "Another headache?"

He didn't answer. All he needed to make the morning a complete disaster was a discussion about headaches in front of Faith. He started to introduce the two women, who were at that moment silently sizing each other up, but Hildy beat him to it.

She stuck out her hand toward Faith. "I'm Hildegard Ixman, but most folks call me Miss Hildy."

That was a surprise. Jones had never known Hildy's last name.

"Faith Kimball. I've heard all about you," Faith replied, predictably excited as she pumped Hildy's hand. "You're practically a living legend, but no one could tell me where you live."

"No one knows where I live. Why would you want to find me?"

"I'm doing a study of the local people around Caddo Lake—how they live, how they talk, what they remember of the old days—"

"You with the gov'ment?" Hildy asked suspiciously.

Faith gave her head an emphatic shake, her curls flying every which way. "I'm working on my doctoral degree in anthropology." She paused, carefully assessing whether Hildy understood.

The old woman's face broke into a broad smile. "Like ol'
Doc Alf. Lessee, what was his last name? Kermit. Dr. Kermit. He was a anther-polgist, too. Do you know him?"

"Do *you* know him?" Faith countered, obviously surprised.

"Well, sure!" She turned to Jones. "Could you put on
some coffee? Me an' this little gal found a friend in common."

"I'd love to visit with you, Miss Hildy," Faith said
gently, "but I think Jones has things to do. He went out of
his way to help me out last night when my tent blew away,
and we were fixin' to go back to the campground when you
arrived."

Jones was amazed at how easily Faith could fall into the
local dialect. She was almost as good as he was. He was also
surprised that she would turn down a golden opportunity
to interview a prime subject for her dissertation simply because she didn't want to inconvenience him any further.

"It's okay," he said. "I s'pose I have time for one more
cup of coffee." He went inside to start a new pot, leaving
the two women on the porch, where they began chattering
like a couple of mockingbirds.

Actually, he didn't mind the delay. The reason he'd been
in such a hurry to get rid of Faith was because of the headache, which Miss Hildy, with her uncanny instinct, had
detected. Sometimes the pain got so intense that he could
barely function, and he didn't want Faith to see him that
way. Aside from the fact that it was humiliating to have
anyone witness him in such a state, the obviously blinding
pain would give Faith one more piece of the puzzle. If she
kept learning things about him, sooner or later she would
put together the pieces of his past, and he simply couldn't
allow that.

But this particular headache seemed to have leveled off. Come to think of it, it was the first one he'd had in several weeks. That was odd.

By the time Faith and Hildy wandered inside to find the coffee, they were trading recipes and reminiscences as if they'd known each other forever. Jones felt a ridiculous pang of jealousy. Hildy had never opened up to him like that. Then again, it was damned hard *not* to open up to the likes of Faith Kimball. She had this way about her that made a person want to flap his jaws.

Jones puttered around in the kitchen, pretending no interest in their conversation. But he thoroughly enjoyed the sensual tones of Faith's voice, which made him think of warm summer breezes and the lazy hum of bees in a garden. He was almost embarrassingly fascinated with Hildy's meanderings, too. She had hardly ever spoken a word about herself to him, and he had never asked, just as she didn't press him for details of his past.

"So you learned about herbs from your grandmother?" Faith asked. She had retrieved a small notebook from her purse and was busily scribbling, a fact that didn't seem to bother Hildy in the least.

Hildy nodded. "Matilda Wilson. She was full-blooded Caddo, but I don't know what her Indian name was. She married a white man and adopted his ways. But the herbs and cures and some of the magic—those she kept."

"Did Dr. Kermit film her?"

"Oh, lawsy, no. She died long before he came along."

"But you say Dr. Kermit took movies of you? I don't remember...wait a minute." Faith's entire face lit up. "Garda Vaughn, right? Now I recognize you!"

"Vaughn was my man's name," Hildy said demurely. "And Garda was what he called me, 'cause he thought it was more dignified than Hildy. No one else called me that."

"Your husband. John, isn't it?"

"John, that's right, but he weren't my husband. Just my man. Ol' Doc Alf figured we was married, since I was showin' six months, and we didn't tell him any different. We was *plannin'* a proper church weddin', ya see, but—" She stopped, then threw an almost apologetic look at Jones.

He was flabbergasted. He'd never thought of Hildy as having a man in her life, or children. What had happened to the child she'd carried thirty years ago? He wouldn't dream of asking, but part of him hoped Faith would.

For once, she reined in her abounding curiosity. "I've caught up with several of the people in Dr. Kermit's films, but most of them have abandoned all the old ways. Why haven't you?" she asked instead.

Hildy shrugged. Her expression became closed, and she stopped.

"I don't have my video camera with me," Faith continued, undeterred, "and I'd really like to get you on tape. Could we get together again later?"

Again Hildy shrugged. "Iffen you want. I have a stand on the highway. Jones can tell you where it is. I'm there most days it ain't raining. Speakin' of which, it's nigh time I was t' work." She turned her attention to Jones. "If you get to feeling poorly with a cold or the ague, just mix that honey with apple cider vinegar, add hot water, and drink it like tea. Mighty soothin' on the throat."

"I'll do that," Jones responded. Her suggestion didn't sound too appetizing, but he'd tried a few of Hildy's concoctions. Some were surprisingly effective.

Hildy took her leave with no more fanfare than when she'd arrived. Jones helped her launch the canoe, then watched as she paddled away. Miss Hildy had insinuated herself into his life against his will, and he had pretty much accepted her presence there, alternately amused and mildly irritated with her. He'd never questioned what sort of person she really was behind the hovering, grandmotherly stereotype she projected. Faith's questions, and Hildy's surprising answers, made him suddenly curious.

He turned to find Faith standing behind him, staring pensively at Hildy's retreat. "Thank you for giving me the time to talk with her," she said sincerely. "Miss Hildy will make a wonderful subject. Imagine, a real medicine woman. Is there any particular reason she plies you with that vile-tasting tea?"

He had his suspicions, but he wasn't about to voice them. "Maybe because I'm the only one who'll drink the stuff."

"Has she given you any other curatives?"

"Lots of 'em. Couple of months ago I sliced my hand open," he said, seeing no harm in supplying Faith with this anecdote. "I probably should have had it stitched, but it was too much trouble to get into town and find a doctor. Then along came Hildy at just the right moment. She gave me a poultice to put on it."

"Did it work?"

"Yeah. The cut healed right up." He showed her the thin scar that ran from the knuckle of his index finger to his wrist. "Then there was this other time—" He stopped. "Damn, how do you do it?"

"Do what?"

"How do you get me talking like that? And Miss Hildy. Usually she never talks about herself."

A mischievous look came into Faith's eyes, which today reflected the same clear blue as the storm-cleansed sky. "Sometimes you have to share a confidence to receive one. Maybe if you told Hildy something about yourself, she would reciprocate."

"Never mind," he grumbled. He should have seen that argument coming. "Sorry I brought it up."

The trip to the Black Cypress Campgrounds was pleasant and much too short, as far as Jones was concerned. Although the waters were clogged with storm debris, there was little else about Caddo Lake to suggest the violence of last night's storms. The air had a scrubbed freshness about it. The gray-green Spanish moss waved gently in the breeze, and defiant wildflowers—marsh marigold, columbine, and morning glory—bloomed on shore.

His headache was all but gone.

He slowed the boat to idle when he spotted a rare sight that would either thrill Faith or scare her half to death. "Look over there," he said in a low voice.

Faith, who had been sitting contentedly in the back chair with her face turned toward the warming sun, glanced in the direction he pointed and gasped. "An alligator! Can you move closer?"

Jones obliged her, enjoying her obvious delight. He'd felt the same surprise and awe upon seeing his first 'gator on Caddo Lake. This one wasn't very big—maybe three feet. When the boat got too close, it slithered off the log where it had been sunning itself and disappeared with surprising quickness.

"Darn, I wish I'd had my camera," Faith said.

"There's a bigger alligator that lives close to my island," he said. "Maybe you could..." No, scratch that. He absolutely was *not* going to invite her to come back. He cleared his throat and started again. "I hear there's a six-footer near the State Park campgrounds."

She eyed him curiously, and Jones was worried that she would pick up where he left off and invite herself to visit him again. She wasn't particularly shy. But in the end she said nothing, which was good. He would have found it hard to look her in the eye and tell her she wasn't welcome on his island.

The scene that greeted them back at the Black Cypress was pitiful. The elderly couple they'd seen last night whining over their damaged camper looked glum and beaten as they prepared a meager-looking breakfast under their awning. The other camper remained on its side, unclaimed. Faith's red tent was still caught high in the pine tree. And the whole campground was littered with broken branches, leaves and flotsam that had blown from who-knew-where. Hoady, who had a big clean-up ahead of him, was naturally nowhere to be seen.

"I can't believe this!" Faith cried as she plucked a brassiere off a tree branch. "That stupid tornado blew my underwear right out of my duffel bag!"

The trees and bushes were indeed festooned with a fascinating array of decorations, including a pair of black lace panties that Jones found highly interesting. What kind of woman brought racy underwear on a camping trip?

One he'd like to know better, he concluded. But that was too damn bad.

With her face a becoming shade of pink, Faith harvested her underwear, along with several T-shirts, socks and one mateless shower thong. Then she looked up forlornly into the tree. "That's a brand-new tent," she lamented. "How am I going to get it down from there?"

He hated to break the news to her, but he suspected the tent was no longer usable. Still, there might be something salvageable left inside. If she wanted it, he would retrieve it for her. He hadn't climbed a tree in years, but it was like riding a bicycle, right?

"Jones, no," she objected when he hoisted himself up to the lowest branch. "You don't have to do that."

"It's no problem." Famous last words, he thought as he found a foothold and moved up to the next branch. With every move he made, the lingering moisture clinging to the upper branches rained down on him.

The tent was a long way up, he realized when he was about halfway there. Were Faith's belongings worth risking his life for? *Ah, hell, what life?* And anyway, he realized with a disturbing jolt, he would risk a lot for Faith. She was a woman with a good heart, a rare find, and he was growing rather fond of her.

He slipped on a wet branch, slid down a few feet, then caught himself. He heard Faith gasp below him.

Feeling pleasantly heroic, now that the adrenaline had kicked in, he inched his way onward and upward.

The tent was caught on a broken branch. Jones scooted out a short distance along the one below it, then reached up. "Clear the way!" he shouted before he gave the broken branch a good shake, dislodging the tent. It hit the ground below with a loud *whump.*

Mission accomplished, he thought triumphantly. Then he looked down and realized just how high a perch he was on. Climbing backward proved to be more difficult than scaling the tree had been.

Fifty feet below, Faith was more worried about Jones than about her things. She poked around halfheartedly inside the tent, but her attention was on his descent from the pine tree. When he'd slipped on his way up, her heart had jumped into her throat. How many times was the man going to risk his neck for her?

The moment his feet touched ground Faith was there, stopping just short of throwing her arms around him. "Thank you," she said breathlessly. "You really didn't have to do that."

"I kind of enjoyed it," he said, shaking his head and flinging some of the moisture out of his hair. "Is there anything salvageable in the tent?"

"My sleeping bag. The radio's a goner, I'm afraid, and the tent itself is a total loss. The nylon is all ripped up and two of the fiberglass poles are—Jones, you're bleeding!"

"Oh, so I am." He lifted the hem of his sweatshirt, which was spotted with blood, to reveal a nasty scrape on his ribs. "Must have done it when I slipped."

Faith winced. The wound looked painful, despite his apparent lack of concern. "Let me clean that up for you. I have a first aid kit in my car—"

He shook his head. "No, no, it's all right."

"But you've done so much for me. You've risked your life for me. I've drunk your coffee and put you out of your bed—"

He raised his hand and lightly touched her lips to halt her objections, then ran his fingertip over her full lower lip in a gentle gesture that caused her breath to catch painfully in her chest. "I don't feel the least bit shortchanged. I have plenty of coffee, and I slept fine on the couch. As for my time... that's something I have way too much of. Way too much and not nearly enough."

She had the feeling he was trying to tell her something with those cryptic words. She stared into his eyes and tried to read the secrets there, but all she could see was a deep-rooted sadness and unmistakable regret.

"What happened to you?" she whispered. She hadn't intended to say the words aloud.

Alarm flickered briefly in his eyes. She had seen it before, when she had ventured too close to his secrets. But he quickly brought it under control. He leaned back against the tree with exaggerated nonchalance. "You don't need to know what happened to me."

''But I—''

''Just hush, Faith.'' He pulled her against him. Before she could even register her surprise, he kissed her, the low boughs of the tree shielding them from view.

She wasn't prepared at all, so that the first touch of his mouth on hers was a shock. Her body tensed and her head swam as if she were on some crazy carnival ride. But soon the initial sensations of disorientation gave way to much more pleasant feelings. Her muscles relaxed one by one, and she leaned into him, savoring the warmth of his body, the hardness of his lips on hers as they branded her with possession.

Oddly enough, the taste of him was familiar. Then she realized why. He had placed his mouth against hers another time, for a much different reason. Then, he had breathed life back into her body. Now he breathed life into her soul.

She'd been waiting for this kiss since the moment she'd laid eyes on him yesterday morning. Hell, she'd been waiting for it all her life. He smelled of clean soap, the scent that had haunted her dreams last night, and pine. She drank in every sensation, wondering how a simple kiss could feel good all the way down to her bones.

And yet there was a certain desperation to the way he held her, in the way his tongue boldly explored and his hands roved over her body and tangled themselves in her hair, as if committing her physical self to memory. She was struck with a disturbing notion. For Jones, this kiss wasn't a new beginning, but an ending.

He was telling her goodbye.

The thought made her heart beat frantically. She twined her fingers in his thick, brown hair and threw her head back, breathing in great gulps of air. He took advantage of the opening she'd given him, trailing kisses along her neck.

His fingertips brushed the side of her breast, fluttered uncertainly, then settled more firmly. The new sensation reverberated from her scalp to her toes, coalescing in a whirlwind of heat.

This had to stop. If it didn't stop, she was going to lose control. She tried to say his name, but the only thing to escape her mouth was a desperate-sounding groan.

A loud banging of pots and pans brought her back to reality. The old couple was cleaning up their breakfast dishes. This wasn't the time or place to lose herself in a man's touch, she reminded herself harshly, although it was probably the only time and place she would get with Jones Larabee.

He caught on to her change of sensibilities and raised his head, ending the assault on her neck. In slow motion he took her by the wrists and gently disentangled her arms from around his shoulders. Taking her cue, she stepped away, although her gaze never left his face. His expression now carefully impassive, the only clue she had of his inner turmoil was the rapid rise and fall of his chest.

If she didn't put some distance between them, she would end up throwing herself into his arms again. Abruptly she whirled on her heel and returned to her forlorn spread of belongings. She could hear the crunch of twigs and pine needles under his feet as he followed her, and she knew he wouldn't make this easy. Well, she wouldn't, either.

"Faith?" Jones cocked his head and leaned down, trying to see into her eyes. "You okay?"

"That depends." She shook out her wet sleeping bag with an angry snap, then began rolling it up, dirt, leaves and all. "Are you going to walk out of my life?"

He shoved his thumbs into the pockets of his jeans. "I don't want to, but I have to."

"Why?"

"Because it's best that way. You have to understand. Please don't ask me—"

"I *don't* understand, and I *will* ask you, dammit." She flung the sleeping bag aside and rounded on him. "And I'll keep on asking until you tell me. I can be just as stubborn as you." She folded her arms across her breasts and stared at him.

He smiled wistfully. "I have no doubt."

When he offered nothing more, she knew this was a lost cause. He had no right to kiss her like that and then walk out of her life without a word, but he was going to do it anyway. Still, she gave it one last shot. "I'll be passing this way again in a few weeks...."

"Don't ask me that." It was a plea.

She hardened her heart against the haunted look in his eyes. "If I happened to show up on your island—"

"No!"

"Why *not?*"

"Because you'll find out why Hoady and the others are afraid of me, that's why not. I'll send you away at gunpoint if I have to." When he continued, his voice was gentler. "You don't want to see me that way, do you?"

She didn't answer him.

"Promise me you won't come to see me again. Faith, promise me."

Even if she didn't agree with him, she couldn't ignore the urgency in his voice. "I promise," she said through gritted teeth. "But I don't like it."

Apparently satisfied, he picked up the sleeping bag she'd tossed aside, shook it free of leaves and began rolling it up against his knee to keep it clean. When he finished the job, he handed her the tight, neatly bound roll. "You have a pretty smile," he said gruffly. "I wish you'd show it to me one more time before I leave."

"You gotta be kidding." She couldn't have dredged up a smile for a million dollars.

He nodded his understanding. "Then I guess I'll say goodbye." He took a step closer, then seemed to think better of whatever he was about to do. Instead he tugged a lock of her hair, then turned and walked away.

She felt the way she had after the accident, when he'd left her without a word, and this time there was no paramedic standing by to take over for him. She remembered calling to him, but he wouldn't turn around. If she called to him now, would he just keep walking?

"Jones!" His name was out of her mouth before she could stop it.

He paused and turned. And because he did, she somehow managed to smile and wave. He waved back as if he was simply running to the store instead of walking out of her life forever. Then he continued on his way.

Six

She had promised she wouldn't return to Jones's island, but she hadn't promised she wouldn't snoop. So here she was at the newspaper office in Holland, Texas, with her nose buried in back issues of the weekly *Holland Windmill*. Jones couldn't tantalize her with all these intriguing scraps of his life and then expect her not to try and put them together, right?

The scrap he probably didn't even realize she had was one she'd forgotten about until she was on the road back to Dallas: the old letter jacket with "Holland High" on the sleeve. Holland was a small town near Dallas, so near in fact that it was in danger of being swallowed up by the large city's suburbs.

She had already perused the local phone book. Not a single Larabee was listed. There was one Hoffman, Lorraine E., but no Mary-Lynn.

Recalling the L.J. monogram on his wallet, she had looked up Jones and found two that matched: Lawrence Jr. and Lyndon. She couldn't imagine *her* Jones carrying either of those first names, but she'd dialed both numbers, anyway. The first was disconnected, and no one had answered the second.

If the *Windmill* failed her, her next step was to interrogate the local citizenry.

Fortunately, she didn't have to take her investigation that far. She hadn't been scanning the papers for long when she found exactly what she was looking for in the form of a six-week-old wedding announcement: "Mary-Lynn Hoffman, daughter of Mrs. John H. Hoffman and the late Mr. Hoffman, was married last Saturday evening to Dan Dinsmore, son of..."

Faith could hardly believe the implications. Was it possible that Jones had given up on life because his lady love had jilted him? But that was so ridiculous! Lots of people got dumped, herself included, and they didn't crawl into a swamp and wait to die.

She studied the photo of Mary-Lynn in her elaborate wedding gown. She was a beauty, with dark, flowing hair, large, thick-lashed eyes and a pretty smile. But was she the type to inspire a man to carry his undying, unrequited love to eternity?

Faith continued to flip backward through issue after issue until she found Mary-Lynn's engagement announcement, just four months before, along with another photo. She was pictured with her husband-to-be, who was a handsome, solid-looking man—but how could anyone choose him over Jones?

Faith made a photocopy of the wedding announcement, although she wasn't sure what she would do with it. When the newspaper provided no further clues, she abandoned the office and went in search of a pay phone. She had to be sure that *this* Mary-Lynn was the right one.

She was being unforgivably pushy, she thought. Brushing aside her guilt, she found Dan Dinsmore's listing in the book and dialed, her heart pounding erratically.

A soft-spoken woman answered.

"Is this Mary-Lynn?" Faith asked.

"Yes. Who is this?"

"Do you know a man named Jones?"

There was a long pause. "Jones? You mean L.J.? Oh, my God, do you know where he is?"

Faith couldn't help responding to the despair in Mary-Lynn's voice. "We might not be talking about the same man," she said, hedging. "Were you engaged to him?"

Another pause. "Yes, but...he disappeared months ago, back in September last year. We've tried everything to find him, but he didn't leave a trace. He's not...I mean, he's okay, isn't he?"

"Depends on your definition of okay. He's alive, if that's what you're asking." And Mary-Lynn certainly hadn't wasted any time mourning Jones's disappearance. She'd scored a diamond ring from Dinsmore almost immediately afterward, Faith thought bitterly. But then she heard a sob that made her heart wrench. Whatever had transpired, Mary-Lynn cared something for Jones, although now was a little late to be showing concern.

"Can you tell me where he is?" the other woman asked in a tear-choked voice.

"No," Faith answered without hesitation. Jones had made it quite clear that he was in hiding; he would never forgive her if she revealed his whereabouts. "He doesn't want to be found."

"Then can you tell him to call or write or something? We've all been just insane with worry about him. He shouldn't be alone. Oh, but he's not alone, I guess. He has you . . . doesn't he?''

Faith didn't answer.

"I'd feel so much better if I knew there was someone taking care of him." There was such a note of hope in Mary-Lynn's voice that Faith felt compelled to reassure her.

"He has a friend," she answered, thinking of Miss Hildy.

"Who *are* you?" Mary-Lynn demanded in a suddenly stronger voice.

Faith got nervous and hung up, although she might have liked to question Mary-Lynn further. Well, it didn't matter, she'd found out what she needed to know.

She drove out of Holland with mixed feelings. She wanted to condemn Mary-Lynn for her heartless betrayal, assigning her with all the fault and leaving Jones blameless. But she had a feeling the truth was more complicated than a simple case of a lover spurned. At any rate, Mary-Lynn had sounded undeniably . . . nice.

After stopping at her University Park duplex just long enough to throw some clothes in a suitcase and grab her video camera, Faith immediately took off for Caddo Lake. She still needed to tape Miss Hildy, she reasoned. She had finally located the produce stand last Sunday, but the hour was late and Hildy had been nowhere around.

Faith made the drive in record time, heading directly to the stand. To her relief, Hildy was there, presiding like a queen over an attractive display of greens and radishes she had grown, jars of honey, small tomato plants ready for the garden, a selection of baked goods and various hanging baskets.

Hildy greeted her with an uncertain smile. "Well, so ya came back. I thought Jones had scared you away for good'n'ever.''

"He certainly tried," Faith said. "Does he make a habit of scaring away every woman he meets?"

"Every *person* who has the misfortune to cross his path, exceptin' me, of course. Takes a lot to scare an old body like me. And you, apparently." She gave a wry laugh.

"But I came back to see you, not him," Faith said, trying to believe it. "Anyway, you're not old. I watched Dr. Kermit's movie again this week, and you couldn't have been over thirty."

"I'll be sixty-two come June, and that's old in my book," Hildy said.

The woman looked closer to seventy, Faith thought as she loaded a fresh tape into her camera. The hard life she'd lived had etched deep lines into her face. "But you're healthy, aren't you? Must be all that herbal tea you drink." She started taping as Hildy answered.

"More likely it's the fresh vegetables. I don't take no strong drink exceptin' on holidays, and I use honey instead of sugar. The tea doesn't hurt, though."

"What's in it?"

"Different things for different teas."

"What's in the tea you give Jones?"

"Oh, nothing out of the ordinary, just some horehound and periwinkle, poke root, sweet violet, lavender and rosemary.... I can't remember what all."

"What's it supposed to do?"

She shrugged. "Nothing special. But Jones likes it, so I make it up for him. It's certainly better for him than those sugary sody-colas he's so fond of."

Soft drinks? Faith couldn't remember seeing any in his house.

She proceeded with the interview, abandoning the subject of Jones Larabee for the moment. Hildy was an excellent subject, though not quite as candid as she'd been when seated in Jones's kitchen. Maybe the camera made her self-conscious, but Faith suspected it was something else. She remembered how uncomfortable Hildy had become when talk had turned to John, the fiancé she'd never married. Today her talk centered more on the way things had changed since her childhood. The years in between were carefully avoided.

Had John abandoned her? Faith wondered. Was that why Hildy lived all alone in the swamp? Jones could certainly relate to that. Maybe that was why he tolerated her and no one else, because he recognized a kindred spirit. It made sense, sort of.

By the time Faith had exhausted two whole tapes, she figured that was enough for one day.

"You goin' to see Jones now?" Hildy asked as Faith packed her camera away.

"He made me promise not to."

"He what? That idiot! That gall-blasted..." Hildy let loose with a string of colorful curses that Faith wished were on tape. "What's the matter with that boy? If any man needs a woman in his life, it's Jones Larabee."

"That's what I think, too, but apparently he disagrees. Miss Hildy, I...I know why he's hiding out."

Hildy arched an inquisitive eyebrow, but said nothing.

"He's pining over some stupid woman who dumped him to marry someone else. The whole thing is ridiculous! I mean, I know it hurts when someone you love doesn't love you back, but that's no reason to waste your life living in a swamp—" Faith clamped her hand over her mouth, horror-struck over what she'd just said. "Oh, but I didn't mean that *you*—"

Hildy raised a hand to halt Faith's fumbled attempt to backpedal. "I know what you mean. And in some ways, you're right. I've a lot to regret, living alone all these years.

But my man didn't throw me over. He passed on sudden-like, afore we could marry. And my young'un died afore he even had a chance to live. He was less than a week old. I guess a part of me died with 'em.''

"Oh, Miss Hildy, I'm so sorry."

She waved away Faith's concern. "I got over the worst of it. But by then I was set in my habits, and I didn't want to live any other way than alone in the swamp. It's too late for me. But it's not too late for Jones."

"I'm afraid it is. He doesn't want me to come near him again."

"So? What he wants and what he'll get are two different things. Force yourself on him."

"But I promised I wouldn't go to see him. And much as I want to help him, I can't break that promise. He would never trust me."

"Hmm." Hildy thought for a few moments. "Tell you what. You be at the Sinclair Marina at eleven o'clock to-morrow morning. I'll take care of the rest."

Jones couldn't believe he'd let Miss Hildy talk him into this. He didn't want to see Faith Kimball again. But he couldn't ignore her summons. So here he was, negotiating his way through the narrow channel at a speed just short of reckless to make the eleven-o'clock appointment.

If Faith had discovered the truth, as Hildy claimed, then he needed to convince her that the choices he'd made were the right ones. Only when she understood why he'd left behind his family and his friends—and Mary-Lynn—would Faith go away and leave him in peace. More important, this was his only chance to convince her to keep his where-abouts a secret.

The moment he spied her sitting at one of the outdoor tables at the marina, he knew that the last thing he wanted was for her to go away. He had never craved a woman's company—or her body—the way he did Faith's. When he'd kissed her, a storm had raged inside him more intense than the one that had ravaged her campsite. And every time he thought of her, which was far too often for his own good, the lightning and wind kicked up again.

He wanted to make love to her with a desire so sharp and clear he could feel it all the way to his bones. But it didn't matter what he wanted. He couldn't afford to be selfish about this.

As he pulled his boat up to the dock, Faith smiled tentatively and waved. Wearing a rose-print cotton blouse and a billowy skirt in a matching fabric, she looked so pretty she made his chest ache. The front of her hair had been pulled back and fastened with a ribbon, leaving the rest loose to form abandoned curls and waves. She was even wearing lipstick. Not that she needed to, but the fact that she'd taken such pains with her appearance for him affected him in ways he'd never imagined.

Instead of waving back, he summoned his most serious frown. If he didn't play this very carefully, he would never convince her to go away and leave him be.

Or maybe he was the one who needed convincing.

"I was afraid you wouldn't come," she said a little breathlessly as he dragged a chair from another table and sat down across from her.

"You didn't give me much choice, did you?"

"Wh-what do you mean?"

"You stuck your nose where it didn't belong, that's what I mean. Hildy claims you know the whole story. I have no choice but to find out just exactly what you discovered and then make sure you keep it to yourself. I don't know how you put it all together, but I do know one thing—if you interfere in any way, if you breathe one word to my family, I'll wring your neck!"

He had to hand it to her. She didn't flinch. She didn't even look scared when he'd done his best to intimidate. She did look hurt, though.

"Jones," she said, and her voice cracked so that she had to clear it and start again. "Jones, I would never do anything to cause you trouble. You must know that. I only want to help."

"Did it ever occur to you that I don't want your help?"

"You might not want it, but you need it." A sudden fierceness came over her as she spoke her next words. "In fact, what you need is to be whomped up the side of the head with a two-by-four."

He couldn't help but wince. "That's quite a novel therapy, but I don't think it would help."

"Well, you surely need *something* to dislodge the fuzz from your brain."

Fuzz? He'd never heard it called that before. "What exactly is it you found out about me?" he asked, hearing the hum of a soft note of hope. Maybe she didn't know the truth after all.

She looked away, avoiding his gaze for the first time since he'd arrived. "I know that Mary-Lynn dumped you," she said softly. "And I know the pain must have been terrible for you to shut yourself off from the world like you have. But you don't have to hold on to the pain. You need to work through it and then get on with your life." She peeked up at him through her lashes, perhaps to see what effect her words were having.

He tried to keep a straight face. Boy, she'd sure gotten her wires crossed somewhere. "I thought your area of expertise was anthropology, not psychology."

"You don't need to be an expert to know what it feels like to be hurt. Everyone's been hurt."

"Yeah, right." If only the pain were as simple as getting over a broken love affair. "How did you find this out?"

"I went to your hometown. That letter jacket hanging in the den closet—"

He nodded his understanding even as alarm bells went off in his head. She'd been to Holland? Who had she talked to? Had she given away his whereabouts?

"I took a chance that Holland High meant Holland, Texas, and I was right. Actually, I never found any evidence that Jones Larabee lived there, but that's because you're using an assumed name, I presume."

He directed his gaze out over the lake where a crowd of fishing boats vied for casting room. He neither confirmed nor denied Faith's assumption.

"Anyway, I didn't find you, but I found Mary-Lynn."

Panic clutched at his gut like an iron fist. "Did you talk to her? Did you tell her where I was?" The question came out as an angry accusation.

"I talked to her on the phone, but I didn't tell her any-thing—not even my own name," Faith replied, amazingly unruffled. "Well, I did tell her you were okay—she's ter-ribly concerned about you, even if she did, um, reject you. She started crying."

Ah, hell, why'd Faith have to tell him that? Now he would feel guilty all over again.

"So, I suppose she told you the whole story?"

"She didn't have to. I found something . . . something in the newspaper."

"What did you find?" This was getting more and more strange. He'd given up on trying to scare Faith away, since it wasn't working anyway. Now, all he wanted was to find out what she knew and discourage her from digging any further into his life. If it came down to telling her the truth . . . well, he might have to. Anything to keep her away from Holland. If his parents found him here, he would have to disappear all over again, and he wasn't sure he was up to running a second time. He had found some measure of peace here.

Until he had saved the life of one Faith Kimball.

"Look, could we go somewhere else?" she asked him, glancing around nervously. The marina was getting crowded. "This really isn't a conversation to be overheard. We could go for a walk or something."

If he hadn't been so curious about the newspaper, he would have said no. But if they were going to spend time alone, they would do it on his terms. "It's a nice day for a boat ride," he said. "Let's go."

Although she wasn't dressed for it, she didn't object. He helped her on board the bass boat, belatedly wishing he hadn't touched her. Even the simple contact of hands brought an unwelcome heat to his body.

Once he settled her onto one of the bench seats, he backed the boat out and took off at a brisk clip. She held her wildly blowing hair with one hand and her skirt with the other, managing neither very well. He caught a glimpse of her slender thigh as the breeze caught the hem of her skirt, and that made him think of those racy black panties he'd seen at the campground adorning a bush. Like an idiot, he wondered what color she wore today.

He thought about taking her to the island, but he doubted he would have the self-control to keep his hands to himself, particularly if she decided it was her role to console the poor jilted lover. Instead, he zigzagged through the swamp, away from the traveled channels and other boaters. He planned to keep her here until he found out what he needed to know and convinced her once and for all not to meddle in his life.

Besides, what could happen in a boat?

When he judged that they were safely off the beaten path, he cut the engine and let the boat drift among the lily pads. It was a still, sultry day for early May, and the noon sun poured through the trees in patches of hot light.

He brushed off a mosquito as he turned toward Faith. "Now, what did you see in the newspaper?"

Wordlessly she reached into her purse and withdrew a folded piece of paper. She hesitated before handing it to him, finally thrusting it at him with her eyes closed, like someone afraid of getting burned.

He had to read the headline twice before he believed it. "Dan Dinsmore? She married Danny 'Dimples' Dinsmore?"

"Oh, Jones, I'm so sorry. I should have broken the news more gently, I know, but I just didn't know how to tell you."

"Man, she didn't waste much time, you know? I wonder how long they were engaged?"

"The engagement announcement was in the paper the first week in October."

"October! Jeez, I hadn't been gone a month!"

"Good, you're angry," Faith said. "I was afraid you'd be really upset."

He couldn't help himself. Maintaining this charade was just too much work, and besides, he was so relieved he couldn't hold it in. He started laughing.

"Jones? You aren't going hysterical on me, are you?"

He reined in the last few chuckles. "No. I'm just so glad she took my advice and found someone else, although she could have waited a decent interval. But Dimples Dins-

more? We used to call him Dimples in high school because
he had two...um, never mind.''

"You mean you're happy she's married?" Faith asked,
all signs of tender concern having magically melted.

"Well, actually..."

"And you aren't carrying a torch for this girl? You liar!
If you weren't interested in me, you should have just told
me instead of making up some ridiculous story about some
nonexistent fiancée—''

"Whoa, wait a minute. I didn't lie. Mary-Lynn and I
were still engaged, last time I checked."

"But you let me believe you were in love with her. And
you obviously aren't, if you can laugh at the news of her
marrying someone else."

He thought a moment before answering. "Mary-Lynn
and I were friends from the time we were kids, and we decided to get married because...I'm not sure. Neither of us
could find anyone else who would tolerate us, I guess, and
we've always gotten along. So, no, I don't believe we were
ever in love. But she is one of the dearest people I know,
and there was no way I could have been unfaithful
to...her...."

Oh, hell. He'd just made a big tactical error. He'd done
away with his handy excuse for keeping Faith at arm's distance. There was no reason on earth for him to be faithful
to Mary-Lynn now that she was married to someone else.

Judging from the speculative gleam in Faith's eye, she
had realized the same thing.

A mosquito the size of a helicopter buzzed her face and
she waved it away. "How about getting us out of here?"

"Where would you like to go?"

"Your cabin," she said boldly, flashing a provocative
half smile. She had him, and she knew it.

"What, no cross examination? You were wrong about everything, you know. I'm not hiding out in the swamp because of a broken heart."

"I figured that out. Would it do me any good to ask you more questions?"

"No."

"That's what I thought."

He reached for the ignition key, then paused. "Faith, what is it you want?"

"The chance to know you better," she answered without hesitation. It was the same thing she'd told him that night they'd taken shelter from the tornado in the public shower building.

The temptation was killing him. Why shouldn't he? he asked himself. Why should a man in his position deny himself one of the few joys left in his life? Why should he even try to resist the temptation posed by pretty, persistent, *nosy* Faith, who obviously had a lot to offer a man? "Are you willing to give something in return?" he asked her.

"You want me to stop asking questions? I can do that."

He couldn't help but smile at her enthusiastic optimism. "Somehow I can't imagine you without a dozen questions on the tip of your tongue. Ask all you want. Just don't get mad when I don't answer."

"I'll try not to. Is that it?"

"No. You have to promise to stay away from Holland. Don't talk to Mary-Lynn again."

"But she's so worried about you. Couldn't I just—"

"Absolutely not. I know she and my parents have hired a private investigator. If they traced a call or a letter to you, it would only be a matter of time before they found me."

She hesitated only a fraction of a second before nodding. "That makes sense. All right, I'll stay away from Holland."

"There's one other thing. Sooner or later I'll tell you to go. When I do, you'll leave without question. No scenes, no arguments. You'll just leave. Unless you can promise me that, I'm taking you back to the marina right now, and that'll be the end of it."

This time she didn't answer right away. She chewed on her thumbnail and stared off into the maze of cypress knees and Spanish moss, as if thinking over her decision very carefully. At least she wasn't being capricious about it. Whatever her answer, he had to believe she would be true to her word.

"It's a lousy deal I'm offering you, Faith. You'd be crazy to take it." And yet he was hoping, praying, that she was a little bit crazy.

When she finally looked up at him, her eyes were swimming with tears. His heart sank. She was turning him down, and could he blame her?

She reached out and took his hand in a firm grasp. "Jones, or whatever your name is, you got a deal."

PLAY "LUCKY H
AND GET . . .

★ Exciting Silhouette Desire® n
★ Plus a Crystal Pendant Neckl

THEN CONTINUE
LUCKY STREAK
SWEETHEART OF

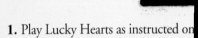

1. Play Lucky Hearts as instructed on
2. Send back this card and you'll recei
   Desire® novels. These books have a
   but they are yours to keep absolute
3. There's no catch. You're under no
   We charge nothing—ZERO—fo
   And you don't have to make any n
   purchases—not even one!
4. The fact is thousands of readers enj
   mail from the Silhouette Reader Se
   convenience of home delivery...the
   novels months before they're availa
   love our discount prices!
5. We hope that after receiving you
   remain a subscriber. But the cho
   or cancel, anytime at all! So why
   invitation, with no risk of any ki

Seven

As Jones guided the bass boat through the swamp, Faith wondered if she hadn't indeed struck a poor bargain. At the time, she had told herself that a chance with Jones, one chance, was all she wanted, and that no price was too high. But would she feel the same when the time came for her to pay up? When Jones finally decided, in a week or a month or a year, that it was time for her to hit the road, would she be able to keep her promise?

She would have to. He was trusting her with a part of his closely guarded life, and she could never betray that trust. Her only hope was that during their time together, however brief, she would discover whatever it was that had driven him into hiding. Once she knew who or what the enemy was, she could fight it.

Lord, he was something. Even in those disreputable khaki shorts and a yellow cotton shirt that had seen one too many washings, he was the most dangerously handsome man she'd ever known. No, she hadn't made a bad deal, she decided.

At least he hadn't forbidden her to ask questions, and now was as good a time as any to get started. She studied him as he studied the treacherous waterway. "So what's your real name?"

He gave her a wary look, then returned his attention to guiding the boat around a particularly tight corner. She detected a slight tightness about his shoulders and the way he gripped the steering wheel. Whether her question or the difficult navigation caused the tension, she didn't know. "It's Jones," he finally answered.

"What's your *first* name?"

"I should have known better than to let you ask questions. If you really have to know my first name, it's Lawrence. Lawrence Jerome Jones."

"Lawrence?" *Egads.* "I don't have to call you Larry-Jerry, do I?"

He laughed at that. "No one calls me Larry or Jerry, not even my mother. Jones or L.J. is fine."

She was relieved to hear that. She couldn't conceive of calling him anything but Jones.

"Are you an attorney?" she asked after several minutes of contemplative silence.

He showed little reaction, seeming to concentrate on pulling the boat into the boathouse. "How'd you come up with that?"

She wondered if this conclusion might be as faulty as the one about his broken heart. "It was easy," she said with an offhand shrug. "You were wearing Harvard Law School boxer shorts the night you slept on the couch."

"And you looked? You should be ashamed of yourself." He cut the engine and stuck the keys in his frayed front pocket.

She was relieved to see some of his good humor returning. "I had no choice, the way you were sprawled across that couch half-naked, displayed for any casual passerby to see." A pleasurable shiver wiggled down her spine as she recalled the scene, and a host of wanton thoughts assailed her. She fumbled a bit as she secured the aft line to the dock. "So are you an attorney?"

"Yes! Damn, you're persistent. What do I have to do to distract you?" He vaulted out of the boat with his usual animal grace, then offered his hand to Faith. She took it, meeting his gaze, seeing the fire that burned in his eyes. It matched the one that was building deep inside her.

"I could think of several things that would distract me," she offered lightly as she stepped onto the dock. Instead of simply releasing his hand, she let her fingertips trail up his arm.

Her brazen flirtation had the desired effect. Jones took a deep breath as if to steady himself. She thought for a moment he was going to take her in his arms right there. She hoped he would. But at the last minute he pulled away from her touch, banking the fire. "With that glib tongue of yours, maybe *you* should have become a lawyer."

Disheartened, she followed him out of the boathouse to the path that led to the front stairs. She couldn't have made her intentions more clear, but maybe Jones had a different idea of what *get to know you better* meant.

She ruffled the soft fronds of the weeping willow tree as they passed. "Actually, I thought about going to law school. But my father talked me into anthropology. He thought that was a more genteel career for a curious woman. Little did he know I'd be slogging through swamps and hanging out with drunks, poachers and other societal misfits."

"So now you've resorted to calling me names?" he said teasingly as he ushered her inside the cabin, a cool respite from the harsh midday sun.

She sighed impatiently. "I didn't mean you. I was talking about some of the people I interviewed for my dissertation, *which,* by the way, will be finished as soon as I edit Miss Hildy's tape and include her information in the paper."

"And then what?"

"A teaching position, if I can find one. Meanwhile, I plan to spend a well-deserved summer vacation with my feet up and a beer in each hand." She plopped down in one of the kitchen chairs to illustrate. "No, change that to lemonade. Beer makes me dizzy."

"You're planning to spend some of that vacation at Caddo Lake, I take it."

"As much as you'll let me." With her bold gaze she dared him to deny her.

His expression grew serious. He pulled up a chair next to hers and again took her hand, absently rubbing her knuckles with the rough pad of his thumb and bringing back those delicious shivers. "Faith, you know I don't want to hurt you, right?"

"I know you don't *want* to, but I have a feeling you will one way or another, despite your best intentions." She tried to affect an offhand manner. "It's a risk I'm willing to take."

"I can't offer you any kind of future, not even a short-term one. There's only here and now. As long as you understand that—"

"I do," she assured him, although she wasn't so sure in her own mind that she believed him. She was falling just a little bit in love with him, and on some level she hoped that she could heal him and make him whole again, no matter how severe the problems in his life were. Stuck out here in the middle of nowhere, Jones was caught in a twilight existence, living neither in darkness nor in light. She was convinced that somehow, someday, she would see him standing in full, bright sun.

"Then everything's okay." He pressed a lingering kiss to the back of her hand. "You hungry?"

"Starved." But not for food.

He flashed that rare, teasing smile. "Good. You can fix us lunch. There are cold cuts in the fridge and some sourdough bread."

How could he talk about lunch at a time like this? Tension was strung so tightly between them she could have strummed it like a set of guitar strings, and now they were supposed to calmly sit down at a table and eat?

"I'll be happy to make lunch," she said cautiously as she stood up. "But first there's just one little thing..." She took his hands and urged him to his feet. He watched her curiously as she slowly spread her arms wide, still holding his hands, until they were standing chest to chest. She turned her face toward his, closed her eyes and trusted that nature would take care of the rest.

She wasn't disappointed. "This is not a little thing," Jones murmured before taking what she offered, kissing her first with a cautious tenderness, then plundering with fierce abandon. He wrapped her in a strong embrace, pinning her arms at her side so she couldn't have freed herself even if she'd wanted to. Her breasts were crushed against his firm chest, and she could measure every labored breath he took. Even his heart could be felt, beating a frenzied duet with hers.

At that moment, she thought she would never get enough of the taste of him and the fresh smell of the outdoors that clung to his clothes and skin. She made a small sound of protest when he broke the kiss, but his intention was only to make a minor adjustment. He held her more gently, freeing her arms so that she could hold him, stroke him, and revel in the powerful muscles of his shoulders and back. When she would have renewed the kiss, he merely brushed his lips with hers, then nestled her head against his shoulder and caressed her hair.

"You said you wanted to know me better," he began in a shaky voice. "How much better?"

"A lot better." She met his gaze squarely, suggestively, making sure this time her meaning was crystal clear. He had to know she wasn't just flirting. She was dead serious. She had no idea how much time he would give her, and she didn't want to waste a minute of it.

"When?"

"How about now?"

He took a deep breath, then blew it out slowly. "We can't right now. The last thing in the world I want to do at this point in my life is father a child."

Oh, so *that* was the problem. She was relieved to know she hadn't misread him. He wanted her, but he wasn't willing to be reckless in his desire. She admired his responsible attitude, then mentally patted herself on the back for her own forward thinking. She extracted herself from his arms. "That's not a problem," she said as she reached for her purse on the table, and after rummaging around a bit pulled out a string of three square, flat packets.

Jones stared at them. "Pretty sure of yourself, weren't you? Or do you always carry those things around in your purse?"

Her cheeks flushed with heat. "I wasn't at all sure of myself, but I believe in being prepared for any eventuality. And no, I don't normally carry them around. I bought these especially for you."

"For me?" At last the implications seemed to reach him. His smile faded and his eyes darkened with desire. "Now?"

Yes, now! She didn't think she could wait another moment. She managed to nod when the words caught in her throat.

"Oh, Faith. Oh, baby." He crushed her to him again, and they spoke no more for a long time.

When he kissed her again, he held nothing back. She responded with a wild hunger of her own, clutching fistfuls of his shirt in both hands to hold him close, her mouth open, her tongue doing fierce battle with his. He rubbed one hand over her hips, allowing his fingers to fleetingly explore between her legs. Her knees went weak. He pulled her flush against him, and she could feel the full extent of his own excitement.

"Mmm, yes," she whispered. She couldn't stand this unbearably sweet tension much longer. She wasn't even sure they would make it to the bedroom at this rate. She didn't care. She reached between them and began unfastening his shirt buttons, indulging in the feel of her mouth against his firm chest between buttons.

His low groan spoke of approval, as well as raw need. The sound of it inflamed her further. She wanted to see and feel all of him. She wanted to unleash the passion that seethed just below the surface, and let it roll over her in wave after wave.

She would have stripped him naked right there in the kitchen if he hadn't swept her into his arms and headed for the stairs. She gave a throaty laugh of appreciation for his boldness, which so conveniently matched her own.

When he reached the loft he set her gently on the bed. Sunshine poured through the skylight in a bright square that illuminated the colorful patchwork quilt as if inviting them to put their lovemaking in a spotlight. In her mind's eye she saw them twined together in the center of the bed with the sun bathing their naked skin, and she wondered how fast they could get their clothes off.

Apparently Jones had his own agenda. Seemingly in no hurry, he painstakingly unfastened the laces of her canvas shoes and pulled them off, then peeled off her pink lace anklets. She wiggled her toes against his hand as he slowly stroked the sole of her foot, first with the pad of his finger, then his fingernail. She broke out in goose bumps.

"Not ticklish?" he asked.

"Not there."

"Where, then?" When she didn't answer, he gave her a devilish smile. "I'll have to find out, won't I?"

The room felt suddenly warm. Again Faith felt the urge to get rid of her clothes. She reached for the top button on her blouse, but Jones shook his head and grinned.

"I'll do that," he told her, and the way he looked at her made her temperature climb toward the boiling point. But she was no longer in such an all-fired hurry. She hoped he would take her clothes off in slow, excruciating steps.

She leaned back against the pile of pillows at the headboard, her arms meekly at her sides, but she looked at him with a deliberate challenge in her eyes, inviting him to make good his threat.

He paused only long enough to kick off his own shoes and, to her surprise, peel off his shorts and briefs with a refreshing lack of self-consciousness. Her surprise quickly gave way to blatant appreciation; the man had a body that should have been carved in marble. His golden tan covered every inch of his body except for a thin, pale strip at his hips. It was there her eyes were naturally drawn. She found that she wanted to touch the rigid flesh that never saw the sun, but her boldness had limits.

All in good time, she told herself.

Jones climbed onto the bed on his hands and knees, reminding her of a prowling tiger. She shivered with the pleasure of anticipation, curbing the impatience that warred with her desire to prolong what would surely be one of the most exquisite experiences of her life.

She couldn't keep her hands off him, though, not when those smoothly planed muscles of his back and shoulders beckoned. As he slowly undid one button after another, pausing to kiss her neck and the tender flesh that swelled above her bra, she let her hands roam. She wanted to learn every detail of his body, commit it to memory and brand it on her soul so he would always be hers, no matter what the future held.

She sat up so that Jones could remove her blouse. He tossed it aside, but he didn't let her lie back down. Instead he urged her to lean forward over her outstretched legs, giving him access to her back. He unhooked her bra, then with nimble fingers he stimulated every nerve ending from her neck to her waist, punctuating his firm strokes with teasing kisses to her shoulders.

By the time he was finished, she felt as if her body was filled with warm honey instead of flesh and blood. She straightened, and her breasts spilled out of the loosened bra, which she quickly tossed aside.

Jones, now reclining beside her, spent a deliciously long minute just looking at her breasts. Then he reached up to stroke one nipple to a hardened bead, and Faith reached a level of wanting that knew no limits. He leaned over and flicked a warm tongue over the rigid peak, then enveloped it in his mouth. His long hair fell forward, the silky strands brushing against her other breast.

She heard a low, soft moan and realized the desperate sound came from her own throat. Could a person die from wanting too intensely? she wondered dreamily. She wanted to rip off the rest of her clothes, roll on top of Jones and take him into her, but her body was seized with a strange lethargy, enabling her to do nothing but enjoy the exquisite torture and continue to let him set the pace.

She heard the sound of a zipper and was vaguely aware that he was taking her skirt off even as he continued to tease her breasts with his tongue. She had nothing left covering her except a pair of white silk panties, and yet she never for one moment felt uncomfortably vulnerable. For two people who had known each other such a short time, they shared an unusual degree of trust, as well as a rare and exciting chemistry.

She experienced only one brief moment of discomfort, and that was when she realized he was looking at the scar on her thigh. "Don't," she said, covering the puckered flesh with her hand. "It's ugly."

He gently moved her hand away. "It's not ugly. It's part of you, and everything about you is beautiful."

She was touched by his words, although she still thought the scar unattractive. "Even the nicks and dents?" She reached up and rubbed the thin, jagged white line on her forehead.

"Especially those. Perfection is boring." He kissed her forehead, then leaned over her leg and ran his tongue along the length of the scar. Her skin there was incredibly sensitive, much more so than almost anywhere else. Her whole body arched in response. Imagine, finding something useful about that ugly scar.

Soon his tongue wandered to other places, including the inside of her left thigh, which was the ticklish place she wouldn't tell him about before. She squirmed and laughed in pure delight as he tortured her with his newfound knowledge. But all laughter died when he slid the panties down her legs and, without warning, pressed his tongue against her most sensitive, secret place.

Before she knew what was happening her passion culminated. Her vision clouded over, and in the span of less than a second she plunged over the edge of a cliff into a raging river of pure bliss, bobbing and diving out of control. The waves washed over her again and again, gradually slowing until all that was left was a keen shimmering, as if her whole body was made of glitter.

When she returned to reality, she was covered with a thin sheen of perspiration, and Jones was holding her. He wore a rather odd expression on his face.

"You might have warned me you come apart at the seams during crucial moments," he teased, although she sensed a certain awe behind the brash words.

"You might have warned *me.* I didn't know I was going to have a crucial moment." She softened the totally unwarranted complaint with a kiss, then several kisses. Before she knew it they were locked together, limbs entwined, mouth against hungry mouth, skin against skin.

Now it was her turn to lead the way. Without a trace of the shyness she expected, she reached between their bodies and touched him. She was surprised to find that he had already made use of the protection she had brought.

"When did you manage this?"

In answer he groaned, and she realized that he had been holding back his own enjoyment in deference to hers. Eager to return the favor, she devoted herself to discovering every sensitive spot on his body. By the time she finished her fevered exploration she was as ready as he was to end the suspense.

She shifted onto her back and coaxed him between her parted legs. He didn't need much encouragement. With touching concern for her comfort and no small degree of control, he eased himself inside her, and the exquisite tension built again with dizzying swiftness.

Jones made love with the soul of a poet. There was a sharpness, an urgency and sheer muscular strength to his thrusts that made her breathless, and yet he was never rough. His attention remained focused on her, looking into her eyes, gauging her reactions even as he took his own pleasure.

Their coupling was sweet and quick but intense. Faith wouldn't have believed she could peak again so soon, but the pressure inside her built right along with his until she was actually moaning, begging for release. It came when he made one final, violent surge inside her, crying out her name. She held on to him fiercely, wishing that she never had to release him.

Jones could hardly believe what had just happened. Never had he let go with a woman the way he'd just done with Faith, and he hadn't even realized he'd been holding anything back until now.

He smoothed a damp strand of hair from her face, and she snuggled drowsily against him, her whole body glowing with the unmistakable blush of satisfaction.

There had been no first-time-sex anxiety with Faith. He had felt perfectly at ease through the whole delicious experience. Of course that really wasn't surprising. Faith had a way of knocking down walls and soothing his nerves even as she inflamed every cell in his body. She had given him the impression, whether true or false, that he knew what to do, when to do it, and that his every move was exactly right. Now he was convinced there was no more powerful aphrodisiac than the confidence of feeling like a superb lover.

Jones didn't move or even open his eyes for uncounted seconds, for fear the sweet-smelling apparition in his arms would vanish in a puff of smoke. During the past hour, the course of his life had changed radically. Instead of day upon empty day stretched out before him, and a lonely bed and sleepless nights, he had Faith's company to look forward to—her shining optimism that was like a balm to his soul, her stimulating conversation and her incredible body.

He hadn't had time to adjust his thinking. For so long, he had asked himself what terrible thing he had done to deserve his rotten fate. Now he had to wonder why he deserved to be rewarded so richly. How could one life be so messed up and so phenomenally good at the same time?

When he noticed she was wide awake and watching him, he rubbed her flat belly with his palm, delighting in the telltale tightening of her muscles. He had never known a woman so responsive. "*Now* are you hungry?"

"I was hungry before."

"But not for ham sandwiches."

"Mmm, with mustard?"

He nodded.

"Can we eat them in bed?" she asked with a naughty smile, curling a strand of his hair around her finger.

The idea had some merit. Faith had already proved she was just as insatiably curious and impertinent in bed as she was out of it. He eagerly anticipated the surprises she had in store for him. He could easily spend a lifetime exploring the subtle nuances in their lovemaking as well as the bigger, bolder aspects.

Unfortunately, he didn't have a lifetime.

Eight

The following week was sheer torture for Faith. She spent most of it holed up in her duplex in Dallas, doing a final polish on her dissertation, editing and reediting videotape, working at a feverish pace. The hectic days reminded her of the stressful life she had lived before the accident—before Jones.

This time it wasn't her deadline, still a whole month away, that drove her. It was the terrible fear that by the time she cleared her schedule and returned to Jones, he would have changed his mind about letting her stay with him.

When she'd left Caddo Lake on Sunday, Jones had worn a thoughtful look on his face, giving her the impression that he wanted to tell her something but couldn't bring himself to do it. Like maybe he'd wanted to tell her not to come back, that he'd made a mistake in allowing her so close.

That worry nagged at her day and night so that she couldn't eat, couldn't sleep. By day she finished her teaching-assistant duties, grading papers and tests, and at night she worked on her own project, chewed her nails to the quick and reminded herself often that this awful state of affairs was only temporary.

On Friday she turned in the dissertation, convinced that the project was as good as it was going to get. Then she haphazardly threw armloads of clothes into a duffel bag, suspended her mail and newspaper delivery indefinitely, tossed everything into her station wagon and headed east.

It was nearing sunset when Faith finally reached Caddo Lake after an exhausting drive. She stopped at the first familiar place she came to, the Black Cypress Campgrounds, and rented another of Hoady Fromme's ramshackle dinghies. She wouldn't have done business with the shifty-eyed little man, but she wasn't sure where else she could rent a boat this late, and time was of the essence. Although she enjoyed the strange, primeval atmosphere of the swamp by day, at night it still posed many hazards, and it scared the daylights out of her. She wasn't up to negotiating the not-yet-familiar route to Jones's island after dusk.

By the time his cabin came into view, twilight had fallen. The crickets were starting their nightly chorus, and the sky, what she could see of it through the dense branches overhead, was a lovely shade of violet that was rapidly deepening to a star-studded indigo. Soon it would be completely dark. She was in trouble if Jones didn't want her here.

As she was tying up the boat, she heard the front door of the cabin open and then slam shut. She was almost afraid to look at him. Would she encounter a stern-faced Jones who would order her away, or the one with the teasing smile, the one who liked to tickle her, the one who lived for today with the zest and passion she so enjoyed?

When she heard his footsteps reach the bottom of the stairs, she finally found some courage and turned around.

Her heart froze; he was frowning. Then she realized he wasn't frowning at her, but at the boat, and she was able to breathe again.

"Did you rent another piece of junk from Hoady?" he asked with obvious disapproval.

"I was in a hurry, and Hoady's was the first place I came to," she explained defensively. "I needed to make it here by dark. Otherwise I would have had to wait until morning."

He seemed to consider her explanation as he helped her out of the boat, his grip on her arm strong and reassuring. Then, at last, he smiled. "I'm glad you didn't wait till morning." Without ceremony he hauled her against his chest in a welcome embrace that literally took her breath away. "God, I've missed you."

"It's only been five days," she said, her voice muffled against his soft cotton shirt.

"The longest damn five days of my life. I was worried you might not come back."

The flood tide of relief made her limbs weak. He *did* want her here. He even had doubts of his own. "How could you even think that? You should know by now I'm harder to get rid of than crabgrass. *You're* the one who had to be convinced that it was okay for me to spend time here."

"I must have been crazy." He tangled his hands in her hair and kissed her, causing her blood to pound through her veins in a tidal wave. Her doubts evaporated like morning fog in the sun.

Jones let go of Faith long enough to grab her duffel bag out of the dinghy and escort her inside. As soon as the front door closed, however, she was back in his arms, drinking in the smell and taste of him and remembering, just remembering, how good he made her feel.

"Dinner's in the oven," Jones said in a low voice.

"Do you always think of food at times like these?"

"I'm just trying to be a good host."

"Will dinner keep for a while?"

"It'll keep till breakfast if you want."

They didn't even make it to the bedroom. Within ten minutes of her arrival they were lying on the braided rug in the living room. Clothes were flung aside in their breathless haste to touch skin with skin.

There were few words and little need for them. Jones explored every inch of her with his hands and his mouth. Her body quivered at each new sensation, and a pulsing heat deep in her abdomen demanded release. That her passion could flare so quickly amazed her.

"Where—" he started to ask, but with that uncanny sixth sense lovers sometimes develop, she already knew what he wanted.

"My purse is on the sofa behind you."

He reached up and grabbed the leather bag, handed it to Faith. "I don't mean to rush you, but..."

"If you don't rush, I will." She fished inside and found what she wanted. Jones didn't even raise an eyebrow when he saw what color it was.

He rolled to his back and pulled her atop him. In seconds he was inside her, surging against her in a delicious way that was already becoming achingly familiar. How had she survived all these years without knowing this kind of fulfillment? And how would she ever get along without it, now that she had tasted such ecstasy?

She rocked against him, clinging to him with a sudden ferocity. She was afraid, so afraid, of losing him. She wished she could just live life moment by moment, the way Jones seemed to be doing, but she couldn't quite make that transition.

The intensity of her climax pushed her to tears. After Jones had found his own release, he held her tenderly, kissing away the moisture on her cheeks.

"Faith, baby, what's wrong?"

How could she tell him she was afraid of giving up the magic she'd found when he hadn't yet asked her to? But she had to say something. "H-how long?" she managed.

Somehow he understood what she was asking. "I wish I could tell you. Days, weeks, maybe months. I just don't know."

"That's not long enough," she said. Years, whole decades, wouldn't have been enough.

"I know. Please don't be sad."

"I'm not sad. I'm very happy, actually. I've never known such…such bliss as when you hold me. I'm just afraid for the future."

"Don't think about the future." He put his arm around her and pulled her close, nuzzling her hair.

"Sometimes I can't help it. It's part of my personality, I think, or at least the way I was brought up. I've always kept the future firmly in mind. That's what my father did, too. He worked like a dog his whole life, planning and saving for a dream retirement he never got to enjoy. Right before he died, he told me not to do that to myself. He told me to enjoy life now, while I was young, because it could end at any time."

"Amen to that. You're taking his advice, aren't you?"

"I didn't at first. All last winter, I kept telling myself that as soon as I finished my doctorate I would slow down. But I probably wouldn't have. In fact, I was already thinking about what sort of studies I would pursue, how I would get grant money, what papers I would publish. It took a car accident to make me see what I was doing to myself.

"I slowed down a lot after that," she continued. "But a person doesn't change her thinking overnight. I still find it very difficult to live strictly for the moment."

"What if the moment's all you have?"

"But what if it isn't?" She settled into a contemplative mood, idly running her hand along the corrugated muscles of his belly. "Remember the proverb about the ant and the grasshopper? The grasshopper had a grand ol' time all summer, strumming his guitar and laughing while the ant worked hard, putting away his stores for the winter. And when winter came—"

He grabbed her hand and brought her palm to his mouth for a kiss. "There won't be a winter for us, Faith. Just summer."

The finality of that statement forced her to realize that her grand scheme was doomed. Jones was very, very serious about the temporary nature of their relationship. It was likely she would never get the truth out of him. And even if she did, it was just as likely she wouldn't get him to change his mind.

Just summer. Putting a deadline on their loving brought a crushing heaviness to her chest, but she hid what she knew would be an unwelcome emotion. She had better get used to the idea, now, of saying goodbye.

She pressed her damp face against his chest, letting the soft brown curls tickle her cheeks and tangle in her eyelashes. She could hear his heart beating a strong, steady rhythm, counting out the seconds, the minutes, of their allotted time together.

She would have to *learn* to live for the moment, dammit. Either that, or her chance at happiness, however brief, was no chance at all.

"Faith, if you're going to cry every time we make love, this isn't going to work."

"I won't," she answered quickly as she sat up and dried the last of her tears with the heel of her hand. Looking at him stretched out on the rug like a contented tomcat, she actually found she could smile. "You can't send me home yet. What would I do with the year's supply of condoms I bought?"

He grinned wickedly. "Oh, yeah. Neon yellow...very interesting. Where in the heck did you get something like that?"

Her mood lifted, and she began to believe that this situation was going to work out after all. "Neon yellow is only the beginning. What's for dinner?"

"Roast chicken and potatoes, which are both going to be dry as sawdust if we don't eat pretty soon."

"You said dinner would keep all night."

"I lied."

Jones knew he wasn't a very good cook, so the dry chicken was no surprise. The surprise was how Faith gobbled it down as if it was the finest filet mignon. He noticed then the faint mauve half moons under her eyes.

"Didn't you eat or sleep this past week?" he asked her.

She slowed her knife and fork long enough to look up at him. "Sorry, I guess I'm bolting down my food like the proverbial pig. No, I didn't eat or sleep much this week. I was nervous, about a lot of things. Got my dissertation finished, though."

"Should I call you 'Dr. Kimball'?"

She took another bite of her baked potato and shook her head while she chewed. "Not yet. I still have to orally defend my paper in front of a committee. The approval process takes forever. And then there's this ceremony with robes and hats and sashes—The Hooding of the Candidates. It's kind of funny, really. You should see it."

He would love to see it. But there were a lot of things he wanted to do that he couldn't—like see his parents again. Fortunately Faith knew better than to ask him to come to her hooding ceremony. He would have hated to tell her no.

"Law school graduation is just as bad," he said.

"Oh, of course. Then you know what I'm talking about. Where did you practice, anyway?"

"More questions?"

She shrugged. "I was just making idle conversation. You don't have to answer."

For once, he believed her. She didn't show the burning curiosity that had glowed in her eyes during earlier inter-rogations. Maybe she really had decided to take him at face value and enjoy their time together day by day, hour by hour. He hoped so.

"I worked for a large firm," he told her. He wouldn't get any more specific than that. It would take very little dig-ging on her part now to uncover the truth. In fact, it was a miracle Mary-Lynn hadn't revealed it. And once Faith dis-covered the truth, she might decide that he'd been right all along—that she was better off keeping her distance.

Even after . . . after he sent her away, he couldn't risk her finding out the real situation. What was more, for her own sake he didn't *want* her to know—ever.

"Criminal law?"

"Business."

"Were you a litigator, or did you work behind the scenes?"

"Some of both." He actually had been his firm's top lit-igator. He had a real flair for courtroom drama. Unfortu-nately it wasn't something he particularly enjoyed. He missed the practice of law, working his way through the intricate maze of statutes and evidentiary procedure, put-ting together the pieces of a puzzle that would win a case.

But he didn't miss the nerve-racking courtroom or the long, exhausting hours. "You about done with that chicken?"

She nodded. "What's for dessert?"

He had to think for a minute. "As a matter of fact, nothing. I don't eat much in the way of sweets anymore."

"Why not?"

"Good question. I guess living this back-to-nature existence has changed my eating habits all the way around. I used to live on fast food and sugar—that was all I had time for, quick, high-calorie fixes. But Miss Hildy has hooked me on greens and fruit and whole-wheat bread." And he certainly had plenty of time to cook.

"You have honey, though, right?"

He nodded.

"And peanut butter? How about cocoa powder?"

He found all three ingredients for her, along with a few others, and she showed him how to make instant peanut-butter fudge. It was intended to be pressed into a pan and chilled, but Faith contended the gooey concoction was perfect for eating right out of the mixing bowl.

"Handy recipe for when you have a sweet tooth and no Ding-Dongs in the cupboard," she said before taking a bite. She closed her eyes and savored it. "Mmmm."

Her expression immediately made him think of a very different sort of satisfaction. He looked at her, and then the bowl of fudge, and a very naughty idea took hold.

"I know just how to put this stuff to a very creative use," he said, stroking her cheek. Her eyes grew wide, but she didn't object as he took the bowl and headed for the stairs.

"How short do you want it?" Faith asked.

Jones sat in front of the bathroom mirror wearing only a towel wrapped negligently about his slim hips. Faith stood behind him in a short cotton robe, scissors and comb poised above his head.

"I don't know. Not too short. Just get it out of my eyes. I had no idea it was so long until you started braiding it this morning."

"Mmm, I like long hair." Especially his. She loved the silky feel of it wrapped around her fingers.

"You do? Maybe I shouldn't cut it."

She was touched that her opinion even mattered. "How about just a trim?"

He nodded. "I trust your judgment. Cut off however much you want."

Faith was no expert barber, but she had watched hairdressers enough to pick up a few techniques. She worked slowly, cutting small snippets at a time and finger combing, then evaluating her efforts in the mirror. Jones kept his eyes closed, perfectly relaxed. He really did trust her.

Faith could hardly believe the spin her life had taken. She had been involved in "serious" relationships before, but nothing like this. The last five days with Jones had been pure heaven. They'd gone fishing and swimming, birdwatching and picking wildflowers. They had cooked together and bathed together. Sometimes they talked until late into the night, and sometimes they shared a profound communion in total silence.

And then there was the lovemaking—always that. She had given her body a workout Jane Fonda would envy, and yet she still wanted more. It wasn't just her heart she had lost to Jones; he had possession of her soul.

But a faint shadow hung over their fragile utopia. There were always the unspoken secrets that lay between them, or rather, one secret in particular that Jones would not share with her. She tried not to think about it, but sometimes she couldn't help it.

He trusted her completely with his body. Why couldn't he trust her with his thoughts as well? He claimed that it was better for *her* that she not know his reasons for hiding from society. But didn't he understand that no truth could be more painful than his silence?

She paused and finger-combed his hair again, finally satisfied with the results. She had layered the front so that it had more shape, but she'd given the back only a minimal trim. Now she smoothed the dark brown strands back from his temples, massaging his scalp.

He gave a long purr of contentment.

"You like that, huh? That's the main reason I go to a salon, to get a good scalp massage." She picked up the scissors to snip at a shaggy end she had missed before, then smoothed his hair back into place. "Hey, what's this?" She fingered a long, curved line of bumps behind his left ear. "Looks like I'm not the only one with a scar. What hap—"

Her words were cut off abruptly when Jones struck with the swiftness of a snake, grabbing her wrist and pulling her hand away from his head.

Her gaze met his in the mirror, and she saw panic in his eyes, the same panic she'd seen before when she'd come too near the truth.

Slowly he relaxed his grip on her arm. "It's nothing," he said, attempting a smile that failed miserably. "I fell off my bike when I was a kid."

The pain of her disappointment was like a dull razor shaving away at her heart. She set the scissors on the countertop, her hand shaking. "Don't lie to me, Jones. Just tell me it's none of my business, but don't lie. I can't take that." Abruptly she turned and left the bathroom.

Jones leaned his head against the edge of the sink until the sick dizziness passed. Damn, he'd forgotten about the scar. He was amazed Faith hadn't found it before now. She had discovered every other minute idiosyncrasy about his body, right down to the small freckle on his little toe.

Would she figure it out? Had she already? The pieces were all there; she needed only to put them together.

Damn, damn, damn! He'd known all along that the beauty and light Faith had brought into his world were only temporary, but he'd hoped it would last a little longer.

When he came out of the bathroom, he saw a shadowy movement through the kitchen door. So he went into the bedroom to find some clothes, giving her a few minutes to herself in case she needed them. Moving slowly, he pulled on a softly faded pair of jeans and a T-shirt, socks and tennis shoes. When he couldn't delay any longer, he wandered into the kitchen.

Faith sat at the table, staring into space as a cup of coffee in front of her grew cold. Jones opened the refrigerator, pretending to study the contents. "Pancakes or waffles for breakfast?"

He didn't get an answer, which didn't surprise him. When he turned around and saw the haunted look in her blue eyes, he knew the party was over. He was going to have to tell her. After all the intimacies they had shared, how could he keep *anything* from her?

"I can't take this anymore," she said, her voice trembling. "I thought I could, but I can't."

"Faith..."

"No, let me finish. It's not your fault. We had an agreement. You didn't promise me anything. I'm the one who can't live up to the terms. All this time I've been pushing aside my doubts, pretending everything was fine, but the fact that you won't trust me has been eating away at me."

"Faith, I—"

"I'm not going to demand that you tell me anything. But I think I should go before . . . before things get any worse."

Things couldn't get any worse, he decided then and there. He had nothing more to lose. "I'll tell you, okay?"

She looked up at him, her surprise showing plainly in her wide blue eyes. "Are you sure?"

He nodded. "Faith, the reason I came to the swamp is . . . I'm dying."

Nine

"What?" He couldn't have said he was— That was ridiculous. She must have misunderstood.

"I'm dying," he said again, unmistakably this time. "I have a few months, maybe only weeks."

She shook her head in denial. "I don't believe you."

He sighed, as if he had expected as much. "Do you know what a glioblastoma multiforme is?"

"No." But it sounded horrible, she thought with an uncontrollable shiver.

"It's a very malignant tumor, and a surgeon pulled one out of my head, just behind my left ear."

Faith stared dumbly for uncounted seconds. This couldn't be happening. "You mean you had c-can..." The word stuck in her throat. She cleared it and tried again. "Cancer? When did this happen?"

"I'm not sure—maybe eighteen months ago. I started having these tremendous headaches. I ignored them for a long time, thinking it was probably stress or something, but when they began affecting my ability to work I had to do something. So I went to my doctor, expecting him to prescribe some pills and tell me not to work so hard. But it didn't come down that way. He sent me to another doctor, and then another. Finally they did MRI—magnetic resonance imaging. It's sort of like a CAT scan—"

"Yes, I know what MRI is," she said, fighting nausea. She clutched at her cold coffee cup until her fingers ached. "My father had one. Go on."

"So they found the tumor, and they told me it would kill me if I didn't have it removed. They recommended the most aggressive treatment—surgery, chemotherapy, radiation."

Faith recoiled inwardly at the thought of anyone cutting into Jones's head. And those poisons. She couldn't imagine chemo and radiation ravaging Jones's strong, vital body, a body that had only hours ago pulsated with sexual vitality as he had thrust into her. She tried to suppress her shuddering, but she couldn't.

"For several months all I could do was hang on. My parents didn't take it well at first."

"No one does, at first," she said in a numb monotone. She was suddenly cold, very cold.

"They insisted I move back home so they could take care of me. Don't get me wrong. I love my parents, and I appreciate everything they did for me. But they about drove me crazy. And Mary-Lynn thought she was helping, she really did."

Faith didn't want to hear about Mary-Lynn.

"She was at my side constantly. I told her she didn't have to marry me, but she wouldn't even consider breaking the engagement."

"Sounds like she was very devoted."

"She was, and it should have been comforting. But instead it was a nightmare. No matter how cheerful or strong she appeared outwardly, I could see the pain...no, not pain, *horror.* I could see it in her eyes. And sometimes, when they thought I was asleep, I could hear her and my mother crying."

"But you got better," Faith said quickly, clinging to straws of hope. "I mean, you're obviously better...."

He shook his head. "Oh, I rallied temporarily. Once the treatments were finished and I started gaining back the weight I'd lost, and my hair grew back—"

Faith gasped. "Your hair!" But of course he'd lost his hair. So had her father.

He grinned without humor. "I was bald as a cue ball." He fingered the dark, glossy strands, still damp from Faith's barbering efforts. "I think that's why I grew it so long. I was so relieved to have it back that I didn't want to cut it.

"Anyway, as soon as I felt up to it I moved back to my own house and returned to work. I thought the sooner life got back to normal, the better. My last checkup was encouraging. Glioblastomas often recur, but eight months after the first diagnosis there was no sign of one. Mary-Lynn started making wedding plans."

He paused, pacing the small kitchen like a caged animal. Faith knew his story was far from finished. She wrapped her bare feet around the chair legs to keep herself sitting down. She was a hair's breadth away from jumping up and running, because she didn't want to hear the rest. Worst of all, she knew it had to be as painful for him to tell it as for her to listen.

"The headaches came back," he finally said. "My doctor had told me before that if the tumor recurred, my chances for survival were pretty dismal, even with aggressive treatment."

"So you opted for no treatment at all."

He was suddenly defensive, his arms crossed, his posture tense. "Tell me you wouldn't do the same thing. I had put my family and friends through hell once already, not to mention what I did to myself. I didn't see any point in repeating the process."

"Of course there's a point!" she objected. "What about prolonging your life?"

"There's something to be said for quality of life over quantity."

"This is quality? Hibernating here by yourself?"

A heavy silence grew between them, and then he smiled. "Actually, it hasn't been bad—especially since you came along." The fleeting smile faded. "Faith, I was going to die, anyway. A few months more or less didn't make that much difference to me, not when I would have to live those months torturing my family. I didn't want them to have to watch me die. I still don't. I'm facing death on my own terms, and that's the way I want it."

"You don't think they're suffering now? If you could have heard Mary-Lynn—"

"Don't talk to me about Mary-Lynn. I've thought it through millions of times, weighed all the pros and cons. I reached a decision, and I'm sticking with it. You can't change my mind."

"I could tell them where you are."

He tensed again, like a hunted animal poised for flight, as panic flashed in his eyes. But the moment passed. "You wouldn't do that."

No, she wouldn't, she realized. She shook her head, ashamed that she'd even mentioned the possibility.

The full import of his confession hit her then. He was dying, and there wasn't a damn thing she could do about it. She had learned about all kinds of cancer when she was participating in a support group for the family members of cancer victims, and brain tumors could be especially deadly.

Cancer. God, if it were anything else she could handle it. But she remembered all too clearly what it was like to lose her father by slow, painful degrees. She didn't believe she was capable of watching another person she loved die that way.

Jones had given her every clue in the world, but she'd never put all the pieces together. Even after she'd found the scar, she hadn't been able to figure it out. Or maybe she had *chosen* not to reach what seemed an obvious conclusion.

Now a lot of things made sense—the way he released the fish he caught, for instance, and the fact that he'd hidden all the animal trophies in the closet. His imminent death had given him such an appreciation for life that he couldn't kill anything, didn't even want to *think* about killing. And then there was the headache Miss Hildy had mentioned the morning after the tornado. Faith had conveniently chosen to forget about that.

"Faith, please don't cry. Enough people have cried for me. I'm not worth that much grief."

She hadn't even realized it, but tears were streaming down her cheeks. "I don't know what else you expect me to do."

"I was hoping you would forget everything I just told you and we could go on like before."

"Go on like before? I . . . I couldn't. . . ."

He nodded, accepting. "Now do you at least understand why I didn't want to tell you?"

"Yes, I think I do," she said quietly, overcome by a new flood of tears. She knew the crying was only making things

worse, but she couldn't help it. "I'll just...I'll just go into
another room and do this." She fled the kitchen with as
much dignity as possible, taking refuge in the bedroom loft.
She was relieved that he didn't follow her.

Jones watched her go, a sick feeling in his stomach. He
had hoped to never again see that haunted look in a woman's eyes. But he'd had to tell her. She'd given him no
choice.

The fact that Faith had only recently lost her father to
cancer made things that much more difficult. From this
point on, she would never be able to look at Jones the same
way, without thinking about the horrors of the future. She
had said it herself—they couldn't go on as before. The best
thing, then, was for her to leave. Now.

The thought of losing her for good brought a fresh ache
to his heart. He had known from the beginning that he
would have to tell her goodbye, and that it would be a
painful experience, but still, he'd thought he would have
more time to prepare himself. It hit him with the clarity of
a hammer to the head—he would never hold her again,
never make love to her.

A sudden surge of anger washed over him. He wasn't
angry at her or himself, but at the whole situation. It was
bad enough that he had to die young. But why did he have
to drag other people through hell? He could handle the pain
of his illness and the inevitability of his death, except for
what it did to people he loved.

He did love Faith, he realized with another flash of in-
sight. Not the way he loved Mary-Lynn. This was the once-
in-a-lifetime love that he'd never before believed existed.
Why did it have to happen *now,* when there was no chance
of a future for them? He thought he had worked through
all his anger. In fact, he had been through all the classic

steps—denial, anger, bargaining with God, depression, until finally he had found acceptance.

Or he thought he had. Right now, he wasn't in the mood to accept anything.

He saw a flash of movement out the kitchen window. Curious, he parted the curtain and looked out. There was Miss Hildy, lumbering across the front yard. Damn, but that woman had the worst timing! How was he going to explain . . .

No, wait a minute. For once, she might be showing up at the most opportune moment. He opened the door and greeted her pleasantly, although he couldn't quite summon a smile.

Miss Hildy looked at him shrewdly as she handed him her shopping bag. "You cut your hair."

"Faith did it."

"Looks pretty good. Where is the girl?"

"In the bedroom. Um, Miss Hildy, I need you to do something for me."

Abruptly her whole demeanor changed. She was no longer her usual cheerful self. "Lordy, Jones, what's wrong?" she asked, uncannily perceptive as always.

"It's Faith. I need you to take her away from here. I would do it, but I think it's better if we say goodbye now, rather than stretching it out."

Hildy looked at him disapprovingly. "Now you know I don't take passengers in my canoe."

"You might want to make an exception. Wait just a minute. I'll go get her." He turned and headed for the loft, ignoring Hildy's sputtered objections.

When he got upstairs, he found Faith sitting on the edge of the bed, dry-eyed but drawn and white as paper. When he touched her hands they were cold and clammy. He wasn't sure, but he thought he recognized the signs of mild shock.

"Faith?"

She barely acknowledged him.

"Faith, honey, I think it might be a good idea if you left the island."

She nodded almost imperceptibly.

"Miss Hildy will take you back to your car. I'll just pack your things, okay?"

When she didn't object, he pulled her duffel bag from the top of the closet and began emptying out the closet and dresser. Some of the clothes he didn't recognize. She hadn't been there long enough to wear them all. He took a turquoise sundress off its hanger and started to fold it. "This is pretty," he said, but she wasn't looking in his direction and gave no indication that she was listening. "Why don't you put it on?"

She did as he asked without protest, slipping out of the cotton robe with all the animation of a mechanical doll. He sucked in his breath, appreciating the last look he would ever have of her sleek body. His knees went weak, and he knew he could easily curl into a fetal position and submit to the same numbness as Faith obviously had.

Time enough later to fall apart. He needed to be strong for a while longer.

When he'd finished packing her clothes, he led her down the stairs. She managed a weak greeting for Miss Hildy.

"Merciful heavens, girl, what happened to you?" Hildy asked with her usual tact.

Jones didn't stay to hear Faith's murmured answer. He went into the bathroom to collect the few toiletries and cosmetics she had brought with her. But he purposely neglected to pack her shampoo. The smell of it would remind him of her, of burying his face in her golden hair as they lay in bed together.

His heart contracted painfully. This was going to be the hardest thing he'd ever done—harder even than leaving home had been.

When he emerged from the bathroom, Hildy and Faith had moved into the kitchen. Hildy was bustling around the stove. Faith sat at the table, her hands folded primly in front of her, her face expressionless.

Hildy gave Jones another of her disapproving looks. "The girl's not going anywhere until she gets a good, strong cup of tea. What did you *do* to her, Jones?"

He saw no point in prevaricating. "I told her the truth."

"And just what truth did you tell her?"

"Aw, come on, Miss Hildy. You figured it out a long time ago. I don't have to spell it out again, do I?"

Her expression grew less disapproving, more appraising. "I thought I knew the way of things," she said. "But now I'm not so sure." She fished around in her shopping bag for bits and pieces of vegetation—roots, leaves, flower petals.

The plants in that bag weren't the normal wares she usually brought. Jones wondered how she'd known she would need something different from the ordinary greens. She put the ingredients in a tea egg and set it to steep in a cup of steaming water she poured from the kettle on the stove. She liberally dosed the concoction with honey, her cure-all, and set it in front of Faith.

"Drink," she said.

Faith obligingly took a sip. Jones expected her to wince at the flavor, but she didn't. In fact, she took another sip, and another. By the time she had finished the whole cup, she did look a shade better than she had. At least she'd lost that ghostly pallor.

"Now," Miss Hildy said decisively. "If you're going with me, say goodbye to the boy and don't take all day about it. I'm late getting to the stand as it is." She grabbed Faith's duffel and carried it out the door, leaving Faith and Jones alone.

He handed her two envelopes, one addressed to his parents, the other to Mary-Lynn. He had written them some time ago, but he hadn't been able to figure out how to deliver them without giving away his hiding place. "Will you mail these from Dallas?"

She nodded and tucked them into her purse.

"I'm sorry." He shrugged helplessly. "I was hoping things would turn out a little better than this."

"It's not your fault. I asked for it, didn't I?"

No, she hadn't asked for this. All she'd wanted was to be with him. And he'd been too selfish to turn her down. He wished he could regret his decision to let her come back here, but he didn't. He would relish every moment they had spent together. The memories would see him through till the end.

He wanted to tell her that he loved her. But he was leery of doing anything that might tip the scales and cause her to want to stay here with him. He couldn't stand the thought of Faith clinging to him the way Mary-Lynn had, out of misplaced guilt. So he kept his love to himself.

She might have been able to see it shining out of his eyes, but she avoided his gaze. "I'd better go," she said.

"Yeah."

"I'll be in touch."

"No, you won't," he said firmly.

She didn't argue with him. He almost wished she would.

In the end, she kissed him on the cheek, then fled as though demons from hell were chasing her.

He watched out the window as she took off her sandals and waded out in the knee-deep water to Hildy's canoe, lifting the hem of her dress to reveal her slim, shapely legs. He watched until the canoe glided around a bend, and his last glimpse of a turquoise dress slipped from view. Then he sat down at the table and bit his lip until the pressure behind his eyes abated.

Faith had gotten halfway back to Dallas before her senses returned. She recognized the stretch of roadway, a hot ribbon of asphalt winding over rolling, red dirt hills, but she had no recollection of how she'd come to be there. She looked down at her turquoise dress and couldn't recall why she was wearing it.

Abruptly the memories of that morning came flooding back, and she had to pull over to the shoulder to avoid another accident. She leaned her head against the steering wheel as her breath came in short, frantic gasps.

My God, what had she done? Jones, the man she loved, had confided to her that he was dying, and she had left him! What kind of slimy, lily-livered, slithering invertebrate was she? Could she possibly condemn him to die alone simply because she was too weak to face that possibility with him?

It's not just a possibility, she reminded herself. Jones had a fatal brain tumor. The thought made her tremble inside with renewed grief. To find such happiness with a man, and then lose it so quickly...

Coward, her conscience spoke up. How could she have just fled the scene like that? True, Jones had taken advantage of her semicatatonia, her state of shock, packing her up and shuffling her into Hildy's canoe so fast it made her head spin to think about it. But she hadn't offered even a token protest.

Mary-Lynn, who was obviously terrified by the prospect of losing Jones, who had seen him weak and ill from radiation poisoning and deadly chemicals, had been willing to stay with him till the end. Why wasn't Faith?

If ever a man needed unconditional love and acceptance, it was when he faced the worst. Wasn't she up to providing what he needed?

She *was*, damn it. She would have to be. If she ran from this, she would never be able to look herself in the mirror again. Watching him die, if it came to that, would be a shattering experience. She knew as much. She also knew she was strong enough to survive it. Her father had taught her that.

With renewed determination she yanked the gearshift into drive, intending to take the first turnaround and head right back to Jones's cabin.

Oh, wait a minute. She couldn't go charging back to him now, not without a plan. In the first place, he might not want her back after the shameful way she'd acted. But even if he did, she was too much of an emotional wreck right now to be of any use to him. She couldn't guarantee that she wouldn't start crying again, and that would make him feel terrible, just as his mother and Mary-Lynn had done when they had cried for him.

The very last thing Jones needed was pity.

So she would continue on to Dallas and give herself some time to accept this dreadful blow he had dealt her. She would also do a little research in the college medical library, and she would talk to her father's oncologist. Once her facts and her head were straight, she would return to Jones. She would be his pillar, his rock . . . maybe even his reason for living, for fighting.

And they would face the worst together.

* * *

Jones was sure there was a buzz saw inside his head. That's what it sounded like, anyway, as he lay diagonally across his bed, still wearing yesterday's cut-off jeans. It was around noon; that much he could tell from the angle of the sun coming in through the skylight. He didn't know much else, except that his head was pounding as if someone had used it for a bowling ball.

He might have seen the headache as evidence of his worsening condition, except for the six-pack-and-a-half of beer he'd drunk the night before in a disgusting fit of self-pity.

The whole week, in fact, had gone by in something of a numb blur. His grief over losing Faith had quickly turned into anger. How could she have abandoned him so easily? He had thought she was made of stronger stuff than that. He had even dared to hope, during unguarded moments, that she could stand up to this unholy curve life had thrown at him. He had dared to hope that she loved him the way he'd come to love her.

Apparently not. With a little help from him she'd run far and fast without a backward look. Of course, that's what he'd wanted. But she could have at least put up a fight, a show of bravery.

He'd found only one thing to dull the pain of his anger, and that was beer. He'd drunk more beer this week than he had during his whole previous lifetime. He figured he wasn't in any danger of pickling his liver; the cancer would get him first. Anyway, he was about ready to give up his brief career as an alcoholic. Drinking didn't get rid of the pain, only dulled it. It was always there, sharp and clear, when he woke up.

Yeah, the beer might have something to do with his pounding head. But the buzz saw he wasn't so sure about.

Jones opened both eyes, coming fully awake, and he realized with an unpleasant pitch to his stomach that the buzzing sound was a boat motor. Company, just what he needed. Probably that thick-necked sheriff's deputy again. He'd already been nosing around once this week, after someone had told him that Jones was hunting out of season.

Jones, hunting? What a joke.

Well, his unwelcome visitor would get an eyeful of him. He figured his nasty reputation needed some shoring up, anyway.

He stumbled down the stairs, raking his hand over a two-days' growth of beard. The buzzing had stopped. Now he was curious, which he considered a good sign. He hadn't felt anything but anger and self-pity for days.

He peered out the kitchen window. What he saw made his heart lurch and his stomach tighten and his knees go weak all at the same time. Faith. *Faith!* It had never occurred to him that his visitor might be Faith, looking abysmally perky in baby blue shorts and a matching blouse that bared her slim, tanned midriff. After the way she'd taken the news of his health and the way she'd torn out of here, he really never expected to see her again.

Suddenly all the confusion roiling around in his head coalesced into raw fury. How dare she do this to him? How many times could he say goodbye to her before it reduced him to a gibbering idiot?

Holding on to his anger like a security blanket, he yanked the front door open and stepped out onto his porch, glaring down at her as she approached, her duffel slung casually over one shoulder. So, she planned to stay, did she? Well, he had other ideas.

His anger slipped a little when he saw the expression on her face. She was utterly determined, definitely penitent, but not a bit sad. Her blue eyes were as clear and steady as a summer sky, without a trace of that haunted look that had plagued his dreams.

He straightened his shoulders and treated her to his most penetrating stare, designed to intimidate, but as always she didn't shrink from him. She didn't give him a chance to berate her for coming back when she knew damn well she shouldn't have.

"I am so ashamed," she said. "I don't know how you'll ever forgive me or trust me again, but I hope you'll try."

Now that really threw him. "Huh?"

"I ran out on you."

"I sent you away. And I'll do it again."

"No, you won't. I won't let you. I'm here for the duration, Jones, like it or not."

He stood at the top of the stairs, blocking her path. "I don't like it. And you'll turn around, get your pretty little butt into that boat, and go back where you came from."

He thought he saw her lower lip quiver, which just about did him in. He wasn't nearly as determined as he wanted her to believe. He had an uncomfortable feeling that he wasn't as determined as she was.

She climbed the stairs and faced him squarely. "We can stand like this all day, or you can let me inside."

He wilted. Short of bodily removing her, which he wasn't up to at the moment, she wasn't leaving. He had only one word for her. "Why?"

"Because when you love someone, you stick by them no matter what. You don't pity them, you don't feel sorry for yourself, you're just there. I intend to be here for you. I love you, Jones."

Ten

The only sign that Jones had heard her passionate declaration was the uncertainty that flickered in his eyes.

At least Faith didn't see revulsion there. She pressed her dubious advantage. "You aren't getting rid of me. You can make all the macho stands you want about facing death alone and unafraid, but you don't fool me. You're scared of dying just like everybody else is, and you don't need to be alone. You don't *want* to be alone."

He relaxed his stance slightly. "This is all very noble of you, Faith, but—"

"Noble, hell! It's what I want, too. I'm walking into this with my eyes wide open. You know what I've been through. I'm a better, stronger person for having been close to my father when he died. And whatever I have to face here with you, I'll be even stronger because of it."

A muscle at the side of his face twitched. He looked at the sky, at his feet, anywhere but at her. "Have you really thought this through?" he finally asked. "When things get bad, you can't count on me to send you away. It was hard enough the last time, and this past week without you has been hell. I don't think I can do it again."

"I don't want you to send me away."

He appraised her with new eyes. She had changed and grown during the past week of soul-searching. She wondered if he could see that.

Finally he nodded his assent, standing aside to let her pass. He didn't touch her.

Well, obviously they couldn't just take up where they'd left off, she reasoned, tamping down her disappointment. The nature of their relationship had changed drastically. Before, their time together had been a temporary fling. Now they were dealing with the long haul. Commitment. Reality. That would take some getting used to.

The inside of the cabin shocked her. She had believed Jones to be a reasonably good housekeeper. At least, she'd never seen anything messier than a stray cobweb or a few dishes in the sink. Now his formerly neat little cabin looked as if a beer truck had exploded there.

"I told you this past week had been hell," he said ruefully.

"I can see that." She smiled, hoping to make light of the situation. The mess didn't bother her as much as the empty beer cans—dozens of them—littering every available surface. Did he drink beer to dull the pain? She sucked in a deep breath at the thought, but that was the extent of her reaction.

She absolutely *wouldn't* show any grief or fear to Jones, for his sake. The last thing she wanted to do was make him uncomfortable about revealing the extent of his illness. From now on, she was counting on him to be completely honest with her—about everything.

"Are you having a lot of pain?" she asked in a conversational tone. She watched him carefully as he answered.

He nodded, then unexpectedly gave a crooked smile. "Not in my head, though. Here." He pointed to his chest.

Faith couldn't come up with a reply for that. She felt a sudden tightness at the back of her throat and had to swallow several times to get rid of it.

"I hurt so bad when you were gone, Faith. I really thought I'd never see you again."

"Then are you glad I'm here?" She held her breath, waiting for his answer.

He hesitated before finally whispering, "Yeah."

She went to him then, unable to stand the space between them any longer. Throwing her arms around his neck, she pressed her face against the lean muscles of his chest, reveling in the musky scent of his skin.

Reluctantly, it seemed, he returned the embrace, lightly rubbing his hands over her back. "Are you sure you want to get this close? I need a shower and shave in the worst way."

She laughed. "Quite sure."

"Have you had lunch?"

"Food again? Jones, you're hopeless!"

"It's just that I don't remember when I last ate something, and I'm suddenly hungry. I'm not sure which biological urge is the stronger, the urge to eat or the urge to...mate." He cupped her bottom with his hand, pressing her hips intimately against his.

Relief welled up inside her right along with her growing desire. Phase one of her battle plan was a success. She was here to stay, and they would find harmony, at least for a while—until phase two.

"It just so happens," she said, "that I brought some groceries with me. They're still in the boat. So while I'm starting on lunch, you can take a shower. You do look a little worse for wear," she added as tactfully as possible. Although the sight of him was still dear to her heart, he reminded her of the underside of a boat that had been docked too long.

He grinned wickedly. "Deal. But I hope you fix something that will keep awhile. I still don't know which urge will win out."

Lunch kept until closer to dinner. By the time Jones emerged from the shower, clean and shaved and almost human again, he'd forgotten all about food. Before Faith could even launch a protest, he had kidnapped her and hustled her off to the bedroom, where they had remained for hour upon hour until they both were so sated they could hardly move.

They finally managed to stumble downstairs and into the kitchen, where they fell upon the corned beef sandwiches Faith had made, like hungry tigers on raw meat. It was one of the best meals he'd ever eaten, one he would remember for a long time.

He knew he shouldn't be so happy that Faith had come back. After being dead set against it, it was hard to believe he was suddenly so accepting. But Faith had changed. Certainly her attitude had changed. And he knew, where he hadn't before, that she would be a source of strength for him, not a reason for worry or guilt. He knew, too, that she was strong enough to watch him die.

Maybe her admission of love had changed his mind. He had never before encountered such unconditional love and acceptance. He had to let her know that he returned her feelings, but he didn't want to just blurt out the words. She might think he was simply echoing her sentiment. No, telling her he loved her required a very special moment. He would know when it arrived.

She emptied her milk glass, then leaned back in her chair looking quite pleased with herself. "So, Jones, has it occurred to you that you don't look very much like a man who's dying?"

Her question had the effect of a pin popping his utopian bubble. Unconditional love? What had he been thinking? There were, very definitely, conditions attached to her devotion. She was going to make him talk about things he would rather keep to himself. But by now he knew that implacable look in her eye. He couldn't keep anything from her. If he hedged, she would stay after her question like a beagle with the scent of a fox in its nose.

Well, maybe it would be good for him to talk. It was certainly easier unloading on Faith than on anyone else. "Looks can be deceiving," he said.

She nodded, not arguing for now. "So, tell me about this brain tumor you have. How big is it?"

"The first one they removed was about the size of an almond."

"But what about this one?" she persisted. "How big was it when it was diagnosed?"

"Uh, well, it wasn't officially diagnosed."

"What?" The single word cracked like rifle fire.

"I had all the same symptoms as before—the headaches, dizziness, mood swings. I didn't need some doctor to tell me what I already knew."

"So you took it upon yourself to assume you had a brain tumor and you were dying?" she asked, sitting ramrod straight, senses alert.

"I *knew* I had a brain tumor. There was a fair probability that it would recur within a year. And there's no assumption to be made about dying. That's a given."

She opened her mouth as if to object, then seemed to think better of it. She leaned back in her chair again. "When did you come here?"

"The end of August."

"So it's been—" she counted on her fingers "—eight, almost nine months?"

That surprised him. He didn't keep a calendar, and he frankly wasn't even sure what month it was. "If you say so."

"And in all that time, has your condition deteriorated at all?"

He had to think about that one. "Actually. . . I still get the headaches."

"When was the last time you had a headache?"

"This morning," he answered automatically, defensively. He wasn't sure where she was going with this inquisition, but he didn't think he would like it.

"I meant, when was the last time you had a headache that wasn't part of a hangover?"

"Oh." Damned if he could remember.

"You had one the morning after the storm," she supplied.

"That's right. That was the last one. You know, you'd make a really good prosecuting attorney."

"Let's stick to the subject, please. Hasn't it occurred to you that yours must be the slowest-growing brain tumor in history? By all the statistics, you should have died a long time ago."

"To be honest, I haven't given it much thought lately. But you can't go by statistics. Every case is different."

"Exactly. Which is why I'd like to string up that doctor who gave you such a grim prognosis if you had a recurrence. He really muddied the waters," she muttered.

"Faith, what are you getting at?"

"I should think it would be obvious!" She wadded up a paper napkin and threw it at him. "You've put a lot of people through hell, when you don't even know for sure if you *are* dying." She jumped up from the table, knocking over her chair, and fled the kitchen.

"Whoa, whoa, wait a minute," Jones said, hot on her heels. "I am so dying!" It occurred to him that this was a bizarre conversation. He'd spent a lot of time and energy keeping his deadly illness a secret from Faith. Now he was switching gears, trying to convince her he *was* terminal.

He followed her to the front door, which she attempted to slam in his face, and out onto the wraparound balcony. He thought she might continue right down the stairs to her dinghy, but she stopped at the porch railing, clutching it until her knuckles turned white, drinking in great gulps of air. She wasn't crying, but he could tell she was close to it.

If she thought he wasn't dying, shouldn't she be happy about it?

"Do you know what I'd planned to do?" She shot the question at him before he had a chance to defend his position. "I was going to convince you to come out of this infernal swamp and accept treatment. I was determined to make you see that doctors can be wrong, that quite possibly you could save your life, or at least extend it a long time, with another round of therapy."

"You wouldn't have succeeded."

"And now I find out you might not even *have* a damn tumor," she added, ignoring his comment.

"Faith, the tumor is there. Those headaches aren't like any other headaches I've ever had. Do you think a tumor can just disappear on its own?"

"Stranger things have happened. It could be a case of spontaneous remission. All the medical journals have documented accounts."

"I don't believe in miracles," he said flatly.

"Okay, then there's Miss Hildy's tea."

"What about the tea?"

"She told me what was in it. Just out of curiosity, I researched the ingredients. Two of them are currently being tested as possible anticarcinogens."

"You're kidding." Since he suspected Hildy had guessed the truth long ago, he'd thought the tea she pushed on him might contain some kind of folk cure, but not anything with scientific backing. "You actually believe Hildy's tea cured me?"

"By your own admission, you were craving the stuff. Sometimes our bodies tell us what we need before our common sense does. But to answer your question, no, I don't really think the tea cured you, nor do I believe you were visited by a miracle. I think it's much more likely you never had a tumor in the first place."

"Faith, if I didn't have a tumor, would I have done all this? Walked away from my job, my family, my fiancée and changed my identity?"

"Maybe. Maybe that's exactly what you wanted to do, and you just needed an excuse."

A charged silence hung heavily between them. Jones opened his mouth to speak but was unable to verbalize his outrage. He made several false starts before saying, "So I invented a tumor? That's crazy!"

Her hands relaxed their death grip on the railing as she assumed a more pensive mood. "Not so crazy, when you think about it. Two years ago, when you first started getting headaches, before you went to the doctor, what did you *think* it was?"

"Are we going to play twenty questions?"

"Humor me. I have a point to make here."

He hesitated, then decided to play her game, if only to prove her wrong. "Okay," he said grudgingly. "I had an incredible caseload at work, defending collapsing Savings and Loans right and left, and they were pushing me to set the wedding date."

"They?"

"Mary-Lynn, her parents, my parents..." The whole damn town, it had seemed. "That's why I thought the headaches were caused by stress."

"And instead your doctor found a brain tumor."

He nodded.

"So you quit work and postponed the wedding indefinitely. That must have been a relief."

"There was no relief during that period."

She looked at him, and for a moment he saw his pain reflected in her eyes and knew she felt it, too. But she continued relentlessly with her argument. "Okay, now think back to eight months ago. What were you doing when the headaches returned?"

"Well, I was back working full-time, and I'd just started on a new corporate bankruptcy case...." One that gave him the jitters now just thinking about it.

"And?"

"And Mary-Lynn was hot and heavy into wedding plans."

"So you were back in the same jam as before. Subconsciously you wanted out, but you couldn't see any way to quit your job and break your engagement without losing face."

"So you're saying my subconscious conjured up a brain tumor?"

"No, it conjured up headaches."

"And you think there never was a second tumor?"

"It's possible, isn't it?" she said, no longer angry. "Oh, Jones, headaches can be caused by all sorts of things."

He shook his head warily. "I don't know about this...."

"It's just a theory. I might be totally off the wall. But it's worth checking out, don't you think?"

Ah, now he saw her angle. She thought she'd drag him to a hospital for some tests, and once there she would convince him to undergo treatment. "Uh-uh, no way," he said, instinctively backing away from her.

She eyed him curiously. "Hmm, one would almost think that you *like* the idea that you're dying."

"What are you talking about? Of course I don't—"

"Or at the very least, that you like being unemployed and unfettered with commitments. Maybe you're afraid to find out you aren't sick, because then you'd have to go back home and live your life, face up to all your responsibilities."

"Now I know you're crazy. Why would I prefer dying to living a long and productive life with you?"

Faith's eyebrows flew up, but she said nothing.

"What I mean is, you really make life worth living, you know?" He reached out and touched her velvety cheek.

Her eyes softened, and for a moment he thought he'd successfully distracted her from this ridiculous argument. But just when he thought she might melt into his arms, her mouth firmed and a new resolve seemed to come over her. "Wasn't life worth living before?"

Damn, she was good. He was glad he would never have to face her in a courtroom. The fact was, on some level he was happier now as an unemployed recluse than before, when he'd been a hot attorney with a promising future engaged to a beautiful and eligible woman.

Was it even remotely possible that Faith was right? That on some deep, subconscious level he had wanted to become ill, so he could use his illness as an escape hatch from an intolerable life?

But if his life was so intolerable, why hadn't he just changed it? Was he so completely devoid of guts and backbone that he couldn't have taken a stand?

Yeah, right. He could just see himself walking right up to Ned Creasey, the senior partner of his firm and one of the most respected attorneys in the state, and telling him that he didn't want to work for him anymore. The crusty old man had given a young, green lawyer the chance of a lifetime. How could Jones have looked him in the eye and told him he wanted to open a puny one-man storefront practice in his hometown doing wills and traffic tickets?

And breaking his engagement to Mary-Lynn would have been a snap, probably causing a major family feud that would have lasted only a couple of generations.

But that didn't mean Faith's argument had any basis in reality. She wasn't a doctor. What did she know? What right did she have to play these head games with him?

"Tell me this," he said, crossing his arms over his bare chest, feeling suddenly vulnerable. "If you're right, why did I still have headaches after I moved down here?"

"Maybe the prospect of dying provided a source of stress—I don't know. The less you focused on death and the more you learned to enjoy living, the fewer headaches you got."

"You have an answer for everything, don't you?" He shoved his thumbs into the pockets of his cutoffs, resisting the urge to run from that knowing look in her eye. Escape. Yet he couldn't seem to just walk away.

She could be right. He wasn't very good at extricating himself from uncomfortable situations. But could his body take over and do it for him?

"I'm going fishing," he said in defiance of his own logic. "Alone."

Faith actually flinched, and Jones wanted to take back that last word. All those times he'd deliberately tried to intimidate her she had stood up to him without even blinking. But one word, one consciously cruel word from him that communicated his disdain for her company, and she looked as if she was about to cry again.

He needed to get away by himself and think, before he said or did anything else stupid.

The woman was amazing. From somewhere she summoned up a smile. "Go ahead," she said. "But I want to offer you this to chew on. What do you have to lose by getting a few tests done? You could find out you have a future, after all."

"Yeah, sure. And if the tests come up positive? If the tumor's really there? Before I know what's happened you'll have me hog-tied and back in the operating room."

"If the tests come up positive," she said slowly, "we'll come back here, and you can live the remainder of your life as planned. I won't mention another word about treatment."

Oddly enough, he believed her. He trusted her to keep her word, once she gave it. "I'll have to think about it." He turned and headed down the stairs and toward the boathouse.

Faith watched him go, knowing she'd played her very last card. If Jones didn't come out of the swamp with her now to have those tests done, he would never come out. Whether he was dying or not, he would be lost, lost to this netherworld existence. Just like Miss Hildy, he would turn in to himself so thoroughly that the process could never be undone. He would be unable to function in society.

God, she hoped she was right, that he was as healthy as he looked. Because if it turned out that he did have a tumor, she'd raised their hopes for nothing. Worse, she had gambled away her right to coax him into treatment. Whatever the diagnosis, she could handle it. Even if he chose not to make her part of his future, she would survive. The one thing she couldn't take was not knowing.

He was gone a long time. Faith bided her time, straightening up the cabin, giving it the elbow grease it needed, then giving herself a good scrubbing. Before dressing in crisp new jeans and a lavender knit top, she donned a set of black lingerie that would knock Jones's socks off, if he'd worn socks. No matter what he decided, she wouldn't turn away from him. It was his body, after all, and his decision to make.

It was almost dark by the time she heard the hum of a boat motor. Perfect timing, she thought as she removed a simmering chili-cheese casserole from the oven. She would treat Jones to one of his favorite dinners, and she wouldn't prod him for an answer. It was a depressing thought, but he might require several days' rumination before he decided whether to accept the terms she'd offered.

She listened with anticipation to his footsteps on the front stairs, the sound of the door opening. He walked into the kitchen, looked at the beautiful table she'd set, gave her a wan smile, then went to the sink to wash his hands.

"Were the fish biting?" she asked, resisting the urge to go to him and put her arms around his lean middle, to tell him how much he meant to her, how much she wanted him to live.

"Not much. I caught a couple of little sunfish." When he turned, he seemed to notice her for the first time. "You look nice. Mmm, dinner smells good." He looked around the kitchen, then peered through the doorway into the living room. "You cleaned up the place. You didn't have to do that."

She shrugged. "I had a few idle hours to fill."

His gaze dropped. "I didn't mean to be gone so long. And earlier, I shouldn't have yelled like I did. I know you're only trying to help."

" 'S okay. Sit down. The casserole's getting cold."

He did as she asked. She poured them two glasses of iced tea. When she looked up, he was staring at her with the oddest expression. "Thank you," he said. "This is really nice. And thank you for giving me some space."

"I don't want to crowd you."

"You don't crowd me. You're just an especially lethal distraction to a man who needs to think. Uh, what have you got on under that pretty shirt, anyway?"

"You'll find out later," she said with a saucy smile, hoping to hide her disappointment. He had purposefully changed the subject. That told her what he thought of her suggestion about hospitals and tests.

He got that predatory look in his eye, and she had a feeling they were destined to suffer through another dry, reheated dinner, possibly around midnight. He got up from his chair and moved around the table, put his hands on her shoulders and gave her a lingering kiss. His mouth was warm and firm, and for a few moments she forgot everything but the joy of his touch, the excitement of feeling her heart kick into overdrive.

She was addicted to the man. How was she going to live without this? She wasn't sure she wanted to.

He held her close, burying his face in her hair. "I've decided to accept your offer," he said. "I'll go to a hospital and have the tests done. On two conditions."

She could scarcely breathe. "Which are . . . ?"

"First, you come with me."

"Well, of course!"

"And second . . . you let me see what's under that shirt."
He let his hand wander beneath the hem of the top to ca-
ress the filmy satin at her midriff. "Is it black?"

Between her happiness and her frenzy of hormones she
couldn't quite verbalize an answer. Then a new emotion
entered the picture, a fear she hadn't encountered before.
What if she was wrong? What if she was clinging to a totally unfounded hope? Had she made a terrible mistake,
meddling in Jones's life, tampering with decisions he had
obviously made at great cost? Maybe uncertainty *was* better than having their worst fears confirmed.

"Faith?"

"Yes, it's black," she whispered, and then she lost herself in the mindless oasis of Jones's love. For a little while,
at least, she wouldn't think about the future. With a little
more practice, she might get really good at that.

Eleven

———

"Why are hospital waiting rooms always so cold?" Faith asked as she rubbed her hands together, then fiddled with one of the hairpins in her tightly coiled chignon.

"It's to make you nervous. And it seems to be working." Jones took one of her slender hands in his. It felt like ice. "Faith, will you stop fidgeting? You're driving me crazy."

"It's the waiting that makes you nervous, not the cold. It took three weeks for your doctor to even get you in for the tests."

And a tense three weeks it had been, too. The wait hadn't bothered him all that much. He was used to killing time. But Faith had been so on edge he worried that she might be creating her own health problem—like ulcers. She acted as if she had more riding on these tests than he did. And maybe she did. She was the one who would have to go on living if and when he didn't.

"We came well before the appointment time," she continued, "and still we've been waiting almost two hours."

"I told you we'd have to make a day of it. That's how these things work." And he should know. No telling how many hours he had spent in waiting rooms.

"I'm sorry. I guess I'm just—"

"Nervous," he finished for her, slipping his arm around her shoulders to rub the cool flesh of her upper arm. "Just think about sitting in the boat when it's a hundred degrees and you'd sell your soul for a cold glass of lemonade."

"Mmm, wish I was there now."

Jones wished he was anywhere but here. He'd promised Faith he would go through with this, but he figured it was a waste of time. Just this morning he'd had another headache, a real doozy. A little stress couldn't possibly cause that much pain. He'd popped four aspirin and tried to act normally, so Faith wouldn't notice. Fortunately she'd been completely distracted by the prospect of their trip to Dallas.

In a way he was glad she'd pushed him into this. It had forced him to analyze his situation, to look at it from a different perspective. And he'd come up with some startling conclusions.

"You know, Faith, I've been thinking."

"Yeah? What about?"

"About your theory that I was subconsciously trying to escape from my commitments. I'm not sure I believe that I got sick on purpose, but I did use the illness as an excuse to escape. There's no denying that I felt some relief when I was able to quit my job and get out of marrying Mary-Lynn for a legitimate, even heroic reason."

Faith's eyes were as round as saucers. "Really? You think there's something to it?"

"Don't you? It's your theory."

"Yeah, but I don't know what I'm talking about. The theory made sense at the time, but since then I've had my doubts about whether I should have stirred all this up."

"Pretty risky to admit that to me before I've even had the tests."

"You wouldn't walk out on me now, would you?"

He couldn't even muster up a good scowl. "No, I guess not. You were right. I need to know, one way or another. And I've decided that, no matter which way it goes, I'm going back home and face my family."

He hadn't thought Faith's eyes could get any bigger, but they did. That must have been the last thing she expected to hear from him.

"By disappearing I thought I was making things easier on Mom and Dad and Mary-Lynn," he explained. "But that was just a rationalization. Really, I was making things easier on myself."

"How so?"

"I had decided not to pursue treatment. I knew everyone would argue with me and try to change my mind, and I wasn't up to defending my position. I was afraid I would cave in just to please them, and the thought of going through surgery and all that other stuff scared me more than dying did. So I ran."

"Are you up to it now? Defending your decision, I mean."

"I'll just have to be. I haven't changed my mind about treatment, but I can't run again. It's not fair to force people you love to live with all that uncertainty. I owe my family the dubious honor of being with me till the end, if that's what they want, no matter how uncomfortable that makes *me*." He added in an undertone, "If they don't throw me out in the street for acting like a horse's rear end."

"They'll understand," Faith said.

A nurse walked into the waiting room, clipboard in hand. "Mr. Jones? Lawrence Jones?"

Jones cringed as he always did when he heard his full name. "Right here." He stood, then looked back at Faith, who wore the bravest, most encouraging smile he'd ever seen. He knew right then that the special moment he'd been waiting for had finally arrived. He leaned down and kissed her, a quick peck, wishing he could prolong it.

"I love you, Faith, I really do," he whispered before turning and striding jauntily toward his date with grim reality.

Faith watched him disappear through the door, then hightailed it to the ladies' room, locked herself in a stall and bawled like a baby.

He did love her. And she'd made a difference in his life. Even if she was wrong, even if he was dying, she would at least know that by dragging him here she'd made a difference. He would go back to his family. He would mend those fences and die without regrets.

But he couldn't die, he just couldn't.

She mopped up the last of her tears, washed her face, repaired her makeup so that Jones would never know she'd been crying. When she returned to the waiting room she closed her eyes, bowed her head and prayed harder than she'd ever prayed in her life.

The minutes crawled by like days. People came and went. One sweet old lady put a gnarled hand on Faith's arm, silently commiserating.

The next time she looked up, Jones was standing at the receptionist's window paying his bill. She inhaled sharply, popping out of her chair like a jack-in-the-box. When he turned, shoving his wallet into the back pocket of his jeans, his face showed absolutely nothing. "You ready?" he asked casually as he offered her his hand.

"You aren't going to give me a clue?"

He nodded toward the door. "Outside. We're in a hospital, and I don't want to make a noisy scene."

"You actually think I'd make a scene?" she demanded indignantly as they left the waiting room.

"Not you, me." He said no more until they were alone on the elevator. That's when his face split into a wide grin.

She could've sunk to the floor in sheer relief. "You rat! All this agony, and you aren't anywhere close to dying, are you!"

He had the good sense to look sheepish. "What can I say? You were right, and I feel like an idiot. There's no tumor, not even a trace of one. Everything tested out completely normal."

She gazed heavenward and whispered a heartfelt thank-you before launching herself at Jones. She threw her arms around his neck and covered his face with kisses. Her efforts were hampered by the fact that they were both giggling uncontrollably. When the elevator doors opened onto a group of women wearing pink volunteer uniforms who gaped wide-eyed at the couple's unseemly display, Faith almost lost it completely. Jones took her hand and pulled her out into the first-floor corridor, and they all but ran for the closest exit.

The moment they were safely outside, Jones let go with an ear-splitting *whoop*. Then he dragged Faith to a sunny patch of grass, where they fell in a heap and kissed again, more seriously this time. Faith drank deeply from the well of his soul, feeling the sheer vitality radiating from him and knowing that she'd done a really good thing by urging him to come here.

He cupped her face in his hand and stared into her eyes until she thought she would melt. "I want to take you home right now and make love to you," he said.

"Home, where? Holland?"

A brief shadow crossed his face, like the sun disappearing behind a cloud. "Tomorrow. Tomorrow I'll face my parents. Today I just want to enjoy being alive with you. Okay?"

"Of course." She gave him an impish smile. "My apartment's only about twenty minutes from here."

The sun came out again.

Faith wasn't sure how she managed to drive the short distance to University Park without hitting something with her car. Jones didn't let up on her the whole way, nibbling her neck at stoplights, pulling the pins out of her hair, running a caressing fingertip up and down her arm until he produced goose bumps despite the day's heat. She'd never seen him quite so playful, and she had a feeling their relationship was about to take on a whole new shade of meaning.

She pulled up to the curb in front of a two-story stucco duplex, which was all but obscured by tall trees and wildly overgrown shrubs. "This is it. I live upstairs. Between my accident and working on my dissertation, I haven't had much time for yard work. My downstairs neighbor mows the grass every once in a while, but that's all."

Jones didn't seem very interested in her landscaping. He stood by the front door, tapping his foot while she fished around in her purse for her house key.

Once inside they went upstairs where the steadily rising heat enveloped them like a sauna, and Faith opened her private entrance. Other than a few dead plants, the place looked pretty good for having been neglected for three weeks. She immediately flipped on the air conditioner, raised all the blinds and opened the French doors onto her small wrought-iron balcony, which was shaded by an out-of-control lugustrum bush. The air outside was warm, but cooler than that inside. She stepped into the welcoming breeze, taking a deep breath of the fresh air.

She didn't realize Jones had followed her until she felt him behind her, his hands in her hair, removing what was left of the pins in her sagging chignon.

"I've never seen you wear your hair like this before. Why'd you do it today?" he asked as he finger-combed the thick golden strands.

"That's how I wear it when I want to look professional or when I want to feel in control. If ever there was a day when I needed control..."

"No need for it now, though, right?" He lifted the heavy mass of hair off her neck and kissed her nape. "In fact," he murmured, "I would rather enjoy seeing you *lose* control." He spanned her slender waist with his hands, then slid them around to her front, moving slowly upward until he covered her breasts.

Heat surged through her, and her knees buckled. She grasped the balcony ledge to keep from falling. "Well, um, I thought when it cooled off inside..." He made slow circles with his palms, causing her nipples to strain against their confines.

"I don't want to wait that long."

A heavy redwood chaise longue sat innocently in the corner. Jones released Faith long enough to flip the flowered canvas cushion to the clean, underneath side.

"Here?" Faith squeaked. "You'll get us arrested for—"

"Unless there's someone hiding in that big bush, no one can see." He was already plucking the hem of her silk shell from the waistband of her linen walking shorts.

She craned her neck to look over her shoulder, and sure enough, he was right. The overgrown vegetation would shield them from prying eyes. Still, the very idea was so illicit that a naughty thrill coursed through her body, heating her blood. Suddenly she was quite taken with the idea. In fact, she felt naughty all over.

So, Jones was impatient, was he?

She batted his hands away, then proceeded to peel the silk shell over her head, revealing her pristine white bra. She hadn't felt very sexy when she'd dressed that morning. Her mind had been on hospitals and needles and people in white uniforms. Having no clue that later she would be stripping down on her balcony to an appreciative audience of one, she had dressed in her most conservative underthings.

Jones didn't seem to mind, judging from the mesmerized glaze over his eyes as he watched. He reached for her, but she took a hop-step back.

"Wait a minute," she said as she stepped out of her shorts, uncovering demure white cotton briefs. Upon consideration she peeled these off, too, then unhooked her bra and sent it flying.

When she looked up, Jones was staring at her with his mouth hanging open. "Faith!"

"What's the matter, did you want to make love with our clothes on?" she asked innocently as she closed the gap between them. Instead of putting her arms around him, however, she went to work on his shirt buttons. "You're the one who suggested we indulge alfresco."

"Yeah, but I didn't think you'd agree."

She looked up at him, afraid she'd gone too far with her temptress act, but she saw no censure there, only excitement and unbridled desire.

He slid his arms around her. "You'd better hurry up with those buttons, baby," he said as he boldly squeezed her buttocks with both hands.

"Hurry?" She gave a throaty laugh and deliberately slowed down. "I think not. We have *lots* of time."

Jones was unaccustomed to this new, sultry Faith. Aside from her decidedly racy taste in underthings, she was usually more on the shy side, responsive and curious but following his lead. Now she was setting the pace, marking their course. He found it incredibly stimulating—as if he hadn't been stimulated already. He was hard as steel and ready to explode.

With clever fingers that trailed fire wherever they touched, Faith soon had him as naked as she was. The warm summer breeze against his bare skin added to his sense of freedom. He had never felt quite so unrestricted. He was overflowing with an indescribable emotion that permeated every cell.

He had just been given a reprieve from a death sentence, and that certainly had something to do with his exhilaration. But most of it had to do with the incomparable woman who was at this moment proving that she had a very talented tongue. Again and again she brought him to the brink of insanity as she knelt beside him, firmly stroking with those long, graceful fingers, gently raking him with her fingernails, nipping with her teeth.

When he could stand no more he pulled her atop him, fitting her against him but not yet entering. The old chaise longue was surprisingly roomy and comfortable, and for uncounted minutes he savored the feel of her silky warmth against him and the tickle produced by the soft gold curls protecting her femininity.

The curls on her head were a delight to him, too, as they fell in disarray all around them like a golden waterfall, brushing his shoulders, lying soft against his face as she peppered his neck with quick, emphatic kisses.

He kneaded her breasts. They were generous but firm and milky white against her newly acquired tan. He traced her bikini line with his tongue, then brought one diamond-hard nipple to his mouth. She arched her back and gave a low moan of pleasure.

"I'm ready," she said in a breathless whisper.

"Are you?" He stroked her hips and the backs of her thighs.

"Don't tease me," she said with a mock scowl. "I'm a desperate woman. I'll take what I want."

"I'd like that." He pressed a packet into her hand. Fortunately he'd had the forethought to bring it with him. It would have been damned awkward to interrupt this moment to go looking for protection.

With loving hands she sheathed him—in purple, this time—so that the act of protection became an erotic gesture unto itself. Then she straddled his hips and sheathed him a second time, her welcoming depths closing around him.

Jones lost himself in the feel of her, hot silk against burning steel. Each stroke brought him deeper into the fantasy that was Faith, her glowing face above his, her eyes the deepest blue he'd ever seen, her lips whispering words he couldn't quite understand for the roar of his own circulation vibrating inside his head. Each thrust he thought would surely be his last, but the ecstasy stretched and expanded to fill him until his whole body felt the pressure, as if he was under a hundred feet of water.

When release came, it was like an electric charge. He lost control and didn't care. Faith was there, his guardian angel, to protect and soothe and keep him in one piece. He trusted that she wouldn't let him hit the ground too harshly.

His conscious sensation was of floating gently to a feathery cloud, the warm scent of Faith all around him. He was dizzy and he wasn't sure which way was up, so he kept his eyes closed and held his lady and waited for sanity to return.

When he could think again, he was ashamed to admit that he'd been so far gone he hadn't been witness to Faith's pleasure. He was pretty sure she'd enjoyed herself, though, judging from the way she was slumped against him, slick with sweat and breathing in his ear as if she'd just run a marathon.

"Hey, princess. You with me?" He stroked her hair.

"Mmm. I think so."

He wasn't very good with pretty words, but he felt compelled to try. "You are without a doubt the most gorgeous, sexiest lady alive, not to mention a most generous lover. I'm crazy about you."

She raised her head and looked at him, still a bit dazed. "Yeah? Does that mean you liked it?"

He reached behind her and gave her a playful swat. "I'm trying to be serious here. I love you, Faith, like I've never loved anyone. Now that I've found out I have a future, I want to spend it with you. What do you think?"

Her eyes grew suspiciously damp. She wiped her face with her hand and threw back her hair. "I think that's the sweetest thing anyone's ever said to me. And I also think I want a cool shower before I melt into a puddle. Would it be impolite of me if I went first?"

He kissed her nose. "Whatever makes you happy."

When he was alone, he wondered what the hell he'd done wrong; it hadn't escaped him that Faith had brushed off his question with a clever quip.

He knew she loved him. She had told him often enough. Even if she hadn't said the words aloud, he would have been able to tell. He could see it in her smile, in the way she looked at him. Mary-Lynn had never looked at him that way.

He couldn't believe that Faith was averse to commitment or responsibility, either. Her whole life was one of commitment, dedication, looking to the future. She had told him as much, and she had proved it to him.

What, then?

He was rushing her, he decided. One step at a time. First they both needed to get used to the idea that he would be around for more than the next few weeks. That would be enough, for now, to keep him walking on air. And when he had his life put back together into some semblance of normalcy, when he had something strong and structured to offer her, they could sit down calmly and hammer out their future.

There was no doubt in his mind about what *he* wanted. He wanted forever, with kids and a picket fence and family vacations to the Ozarks, and Faith right at the center. She had already become such an integral part of his existence that he couldn't imagine life without her.

He had saved her life, and she had saved his by dragging him away from the swamp before he became the bitter, isolated man he was pretending to be. It just seemed right that they should spend their salvaged lives together.

Faith pressed her face against the cool tile wall as tepid water washed over her, mingling with her tears. She hadn't expected a marriage proposal, or anything even resembling one, and Jones's question had caused panic to rise up in her throat like a tidal wave.

She thought she had handled it well, pretending not to take him seriously. But he *had* been serious, at least at the time. She could only hope that, upon reflection, he would realize he didn't really want to be married, and he would be glad she hadn't jumped at the chance to bind herself to him for eternity.

It wasn't that she didn't want to be his wife. In fact, the idea held considerable appeal. Before, she hadn't allowed herself to dwell on the idea because it wasn't within the realm of possibility. Now she couldn't help herself.

They could be good together, she thought. They had already learned so much from each other, and she had to believe they would continue to stretch and grow, even though circumstances had changed.

And the children. Jones would be a wonderful father, patient and gentle, passing on his compassion and his finely honed respect for all life. She would dearly love to bear his children.

But it wasn't to be, not in this lifetime. Jones had demonstrated, quite convincingly, that marriage wasn't in his best interest. His subconscious dread of his approaching nuptials with Mary-Lynn had almost destroyed his life. Faith wouldn't doom him to that fate again, no matter how easily an impulsive marriage proposal tripped off his tongue.

If not marriage, what could the future hold for them? she wondered. Certainly their idyllic time together at Caddo Lake, filling hour after lazy hour with whatever activities took their fancy, was over. She had a career to launch, and he had a family to get reacquainted with, a life to put back together.

She hadn't thought about all these consequences before; all she'd wanted was to get Jones to a doctor, and she hadn't looked past that goal.

Suddenly the future appeared to be a black, mysterious void. She couldn't marry him, but she sure as hell didn't want to lose him. Was there a middle ground?

She definitely should have looked ahead before now. This business of living one day at a time could get to be a bad habit.

Twelve

Faith stared in amazement at the mansion that rose before her, resplendent white on white. Huge columns that would do justice to a national government building supported a three-tiered front porch that looked as if it had been carved from marble, something straight out of *Gone with the Wind*. The red brick driveway circled around a fountain that sported bronze statues of life-size horses and mythological tritons.

"Your parents aren't by any chance the richest people in town, are they?"

"Possibly," Jones answered, preoccupied. "Might be the Hoffmans, though."

"As in Mary-Lynn? I should have known. How are you going to explain me to people who are used to seeing you with the most eligible girl in town?" It had never occurred to her that Jones, or at least his parents, fell in the millionaire category. Millionaires tended to look down their noses at penniless, jobless nobodies like herself with wild hair and clothes bought off sale racks and at consignment stores. Here was another good reason she couldn't accept his impulsive plans for the future.

"I won't have to explain you, except to say you're a close friend. Don't worry, they're very accepting."

But they would know she and Jones were involved, Faith thought. Parents could always sense that sort of thing. Jones's folks would probably assume she'd had something to do with their son's disappearance—that she had talked him into running off with her. But she didn't voice these doubts. Jones had enough to worry about. What did it matter if she made a bad impression on his folks?

She probably would never see them again. She was with Jones today for moral support as he faced his last big hurdle. Afterward...who knew? Ever since her blithe dismissal of his proposal, a subtle tension had lain between them.

"Maybe we should have called," she said as they got out of the car. "Your folks haven't seen you in almost a year. You're bound to scare the living daylights out of them."

"They'll get over it. Besides, I didn't want to give them any warning. That would only have allowed them time to work up a good rage over the fact that I've put them through hell for nothing."

"You did what you thought was right at the time," Faith said, squeezing his hand. "Don't beat yourself up over it now. I'm sure everyone will understand. And they'll be so happy you're home they won't be mad. The Prodigal Son and all that."

"If you say so." He hesitated, then rang the bell.

"You ring the bell at your own parents' house?"

"They aren't expecting me," he explained, as if etiquette were a main concern here.

"I'll say," she mumbled.

The woman who answered the door was sixtyish and quite pretty in a tall, commanding way. She wore a perfectly unwrinkled, belted linen dress, off-white stockings, and bone-colored pumps. Her dark hair, laced with artful streaks of silver, was swept back at the nape with a silk scarf. Her understated makeup enhanced perfectly sculpted cheekbones, an aristocratic nose and a mouth set in a pleasant but distant smile. She even wore a string of pearls.

June Cleaver, all grown up, Faith thought irreverently as the other woman's face lit up with recognition and all semblance of dignity vanished.

"L.J.!" she shrieked just before her eyes rolled back into her head and she fell in an inelegant heap on the entry hall floor.

"Mom!" Jones dived for her, saving her from hitting her head on the marble tiles.

Faith made a flying leap through the doorway, intent on finding some water to revive poor Mrs. Jones. A woman in a maid's uniform skidded to a halt in the entryway at the same instant. She crossed herself, then began an endless tirade in Spanish that, although Faith could understand only a few words, had something to do with calling the police.

Fortunately Mrs. Jones came to and prevented the maid from carrying out her threat.

"For heaven's sake, Juanita, stop jabbering," she said muzzily as Jones helped her to her feet. "It's not a robbery, it's my son." She paused, staring at Jones up and down. "What do you mean, showing up like this without warning after almost a year, and only one lousy letter? We thought you were dead!"

Jeez, Faith thought, instinctively backing away from the termagant, no wonder Jones had been so apprehensive about coming home. Didn't this woman have even an ounce of motherly love?

"I guess I have some explaining to do," Jones said, sounding like a teenager who had dented the fender on the family station wagon. Or maybe the Rolls Royce, in this family.

"You certainly do." Abruptly her outrage faded and her face crumpled. "Oh, what's the matter with me? I can't believe you're here, you're alive!"

Finally Faith detected a tear in the older woman's eye. She threw her arms around her son, and Jones returned the embrace. Yes, this was more as it should be.

Mrs. Jones's show of emotion was brief, however. "Your father is going to have a coronary," she said, recovering quickly with a few delicate sniffs. "It's a good thing he's not home. Now I can break the news to him gently. Gracious, I have to call him at the club."

"Mom, before you do that, I'd like you to meet someone very special. This is Faith Kimball. She has a lot to do with why I'm standing here right now."

Faith would just as soon have faded into the background as withstand the formidable stare of Mrs. Jones, who after a brief inspection, crisply extended her hand. "It's nice to meet you, Ms. Kimball."

"Call me Faith, please."

Mrs. Jones nodded but didn't counter with a similar invitation of familiarity. "Your father," she said, returning her attention to Jones. "I have to call him right away." She led the way out of the entry hall, the startled maid still looking on, and headed into a central room that Faith could only describe as a "great hall."

"And Mary-Lynn," Mrs. Jones continued. "She was a wreck after you left without a word. She was so distraught she—'' The sentence was cut off abruptly. ''Oh, my, you probably don't know about Mary-Lynn, do you.''

''That she married Dimples Dinsmore, you mean? Yeah, and I think it's the best thing that could have happened.''

''You do? Well...'' She pursed her lips and frowned. ''We didn't much approve of it, you know. When she accepted Dan's proposal, the whole town said she was out of her mind, crazy over losing you, and that she would come to her senses before the wedding, but she didn't. Her father still will hardly speak to her. He's always been so enamored with the idea of joining the Joneses and the Hoffmans and starting an empire. I must say, your father and I were counting on it, too—''

''Mom,'' Jones interrupted with an uncomfortable glance toward Faith, ''we can talk about that later. Just call Dad.''

Mrs. Jones picked up the French Provincial phone. ''Oh, dear, the judge does so *hate* having his golf game interrupted.''

The afternoon went downhill from there. It wasn't that the elder Joneses were nasty people. They were actually rather nice, warming up to Faith when they discovered her role in their son's ''recovery.'' They seemed duly impressed, too, that she was just weeks away from receiving her doctoral degree. They didn't grill her or Jones about their relationship—at least, not right away—which was fine with her since neither of them would have had a very definitive answer.

But ''the judge'' and Mrs. Jones—no first names were forthcoming—were the stiffest, most formally correct people Faith had ever encountered. Not even in the realm of academia had she known one person who actually *dressed* for dinner, or wore pearls in the afternoon, for that matter.

No wonder Jones had learned to internalize his stress. As the day wore on, it became more and more clear that he had spent his entire life trying to please these people, whom he obviously adored, and that they were very, very difficult to please. Although they were glad he was hale and hearty and with them again, they were peeved over his unnecessary disappearance, and they didn't fail to let him know.

"You've done irreparable damage to your career, you know," his father grumbled during their five-course dinner, complete with three different wines. "You can't just take off a year and then expect to pick up where you left off."

"I realize that," Jones said good-naturedly.

The judge gingerly wiped his mouth with a napkin. "I'll talk to old man Creasey. He's the senior partner in L.J.'s firm," he explained in an aside to Faith.

"That's not necessary." Jones cut into a piece of meat with more zeal than the tender beef warranted. "I'll talk to him myself. The firm always needs good litigators. They'll probably cut my salary, but they wouldn't turn me down."

Faith nearly choked on her steak. He was kidding, wasn't he?

"You'll cut your hair first, I trust," Mrs. Jones said with another of her disapproving frowns. She had honed that expression to a fine art.

Faith bit her lip to keep from making an unwelcome comment. She liked Jones's hair just fine the way it was.

When the interminable dinner finally ended, Faith half expected the men to retire to the library for brandy and cigars. Such a gesture would have suited the anachronistic meal. Fortunately, they never got the chance. The doorbell chimed, and moments later a gorgeous brunette glided into the dining room and threw herself into Jones's arms.

"Oh, L.J., L.J., it really *is* you," she wailed, and then she gave him a smacker right on the mouth.

He actually blushed. "Uh, hi, Mary-Lynn."

Mrs. Jones grabbed Faith's arm. "Why don't we go out onto the patio?" she said, steering Faith none too gently toward a set of French doors. She turned toward her husband. "Lawrence?" It was the first time Faith had heard his first name. She still didn't know Mrs. Jones's. "Let's show Faith your bonsai tree collection."

And leave the tragically separated lovers to their touching reunion, Faith added silently. Jones gave her a pleading look, as if to say that events had escalated entirely out of his control, as they apparently had. She nodded her understanding despite the stab of jealousy she felt at seeing his former fiancée plastered to him like a fried egg stuck to a pan.

"So," Mrs. Jones said after Faith had taken the bonsai tour and Lawrence Jones, Sr., had tactfully faded away. "I'm just curious... er, what is the nature of your friendship with L.J.? Is it a serious sort of thing?"

"Yes," Faith replied without hesitation. She wouldn't trivialize her feelings for Jones, not even to keep the peace. "But you don't have to worry. I don't intend to marry him."

"Oh. Well, that's a relief. Not that there's anything wrong with you, my dear," she added hastily. "I'm sure you're a perfectly nice girl. But after the ordeal L.J. has been through, I feel he needs some time to get his life settled before he plunges into anything."

"I couldn't agree with you more," Faith said. For once, she and Mrs. Jones were in accord.

When Jones came out on the patio, he was alone.

"What happened to Mary-Lynn?" his mother asked.

"She went home. To her husband," he said, emphasizing the last word. He was clearly displeased. "And Faith and I have to be going, too."

"You mean you aren't staying here?" The older woman's hand fluttered at her throat.

"No. I'm spending the night in Dallas," he said, and Faith was relieved that at least he hadn't revealed he would be sleeping in her apartment. "I'll be opening up my house in the next few days, though, so I'll be back soon. Tell Dad goodbye for me." He kissed her on the cheek, and with blessed haste he and Faith made their escape.

"You have lipstick on your chin," Faith said when they were alone in the car. "And it's definitely not my shade."

"Mmm." He rubbed ineffectually at the stain. "You jealous?"

"How am I supposed to feel when I see a gorgeous woman with legs up to her armpits throw herself at you and kiss you right on the mouth?"

"She was . . . overcome."

"What did you talk about?"

"Trust me, it wasn't pleasant. She let me have it with both barrels for making her worry about me for no good reason, and I reminded her that she'd worried herself right into the arms of another man. Then she got all defensive and started grilling me about you. She actually accused *me* of being unfaithful, can you believe that?"

"No, I really can't," Faith murmured, frankly astonished. "I thought you were crazy to worry about how your family and friends would greet your return. I was sure they would be so happy you're okay, and so touched by what you tried to do, that all would be forgiven. But your parents did nothing but criticize, and your beloved fiancée—"

"Former beloved fiancée," he corrected her.

"Whatever. Apparently all she could focus on was her own petty suffering. She'll never appreciate what you went through. You *were* faithful to her, up until you found out she was married."

"At great cost, I might add," he said, running his fingers lightly down Faith's arm before starting the car. "Ah, Faith, I'm really sorry about this whole day. Here I was, trying to convince you of what nice in-laws they would make, and my parents have never behaved more miserably."

In-laws. Well, it looked as if she couldn't duck the issue much longer. His mother had given Faith a good line of defense. She might be able to squeak by this marriage issue without destroying the whole relationship. Still, her palms grew damp at the thought of disguising her true feelings, even if it was for his own good.

They said nothing more until they were inside Faith's apartment. That's when she noticed the lines in his forehead and the tight way he held his mouth. "Do you have a headache?" she asked. It wouldn't surprise her. Mr. and Mrs. Jones could give anyone a headache.

"Just the start of one. What's in your medicine cabinet?"

She took his hand and led him to the couch. "Forget the pills. You said they don't do much good anyway. Let's try something else. Stretch out and put your head in my lap."

He gave her a dubious look, but he took his shoes off and complied with her order.

She began a slow massage of his neck, and then his temples. When his eyelids fluttered closed, she began talking. She guided him through a progressive relaxation exercise she'd learned with her father, starting with his toes and working up to his scalp. "Now, imagine you're fishing," she said. "The boat is anchored in a nice, sunny spot, your line's in the water, and you have a cooler full of Miss Hildy's tea on ice. The sun is shining down, warming your skin, a soft breeze is blowing...."

"Are you fishing, too?" he asked drowsily.

"If you want me to be."

"Definitely."

She felt irrationally pleased by his response. "Okay. The sun is shining, the breeze is blowing—"

"Faith, don't you want to marry me?"

She sighed as their languid mood dissipated. "Oh, Jones, there are so many changes going on in our lives right now. I have my graduation to think about—I still have to do my interview before the committee, you know. And then I have to think about getting a job. And you have to start your life all over again. You have a lot of decisions to make, and getting married shouldn't be one of them. You could use some time to yourself, to—"

He sat up suddenly, raking his hand through his disheveled hair. "Time to myself? I've had about all of that I can stand, thanks. Faith, I thought you loved me. You said you did. Or was that just a platitude to soothe a dying man?"

"Of course I love you," she shot back, alarmed that he would think, even for a minute, that she had manufactured her feelings out of pity. She couldn't possibly lie about that. "I just feel this is a bad time for either one of us to discuss settling down. I mean, this is forever we're talking about."

A funny look came into Jones's eyes, and it scared her. "Oh, now I get it," he said with a curious flatness to his voice. "You said you'd be with me for the duration, but that was when you didn't know how long the duration would be."

"Now, wait a minute—"

"All this time, I thought you were committed to me, but now I see. I was just a 'cause' for you, another study in human behavior. 'Survival Tactics of the Terminally Ill.' Has a nice ring to it."

"Don't say such awful things! I never for one minute—"

"Well, sorry I've inconvenienced you by not dying. But don't let me interfere with your precious career plans." He stood and started for the door.

"Where are you going?"

"To a hotel, where I can nurse my headache in peace."

"Oh, no, you don't," she said, scooting in front of him and barring the door. "You can't accuse me of something like that and then leave without giving me a chance to defend myself."

He folded his arms, leaned back against the wall, and crossed his long legs at the ankle. "I'd like to hear you defend yourself. Come on, put that golden tongue of yours to work."

She threw up her hands in resignation. "You don't sound as if you'll believe anything I tell you, now. Hell, I should have known better than to offer you anything but the whole truth. I wanted to give you a chance to see it for yourself, but..."

"See what?"

"You really don't get it, do you? It's the stress, Jones. Stress almost killed you. It gives you headaches, and it might have contributed to the brain tumor, too. Doctors are only now beginning to investigate the connection between stress and cancer. You removed the stress from your life, and you started feeling better. Are you with me so far?"

His nod of agreement was almost imperceptible.

"Now, you've known you aren't dying for, what, a little more than twenty-four hours? And you're scrambling as fast as you can to get exactly where you were when you got sick. You've promised your father you'll talk to that Creasey person about getting your old job back, and you're trying to get engaged—the two main things that made your life so unlivable you willingly faced death to escape.

"I was willing to watch you die when I thought you had no choice. But, buster, you have a choice, now, and I will *not* stand idly by and watch you kill yourself, and I especially won't be part of the poison."

He paled beneath his tan as the smug, self-righteous anger seemed to drain out of him. He turned and walked unsteadily to the couch, then sank onto it.

Faith followed him quietly, watching but not wanting to get in the way. Her blunt assessment had apparently hit its mark; Jones's jaw worked furiously as he stared at the opposite wall, unseeing, working through something.

"My God, Faith, you're right," he finally said. "It's all so automatic, so ingrained. I was just doing what I was programmed to do—like all those months at Caddo meant nothing. Didn't I learn anything?"

"I don't know, did you?"

"I'd like to think I did, but it's amazing how easy it is to fall back into familiar patterns. Pretty soon I probably would have started eating junk food and quit exercising, too."

She remained quiet. This was something he would have to work out on his own—just as she had worked it out for herself after the accident.

"But if I don't take back my old job, what do I do? I was educated at one of the best law schools, and personally trained by one of the best lawyers in the country. I can't turn my back on that."

"Why not, if you don't like it?"

"And do what? Be a bum? I couldn't live my life like that. Even fishing and swimming all the time would get boring after a while."

"You seemed to like it all right before."

"That's because I thought I didn't have much time. I have to *do* something with my life. I can't just waste it."

"Then do something you *want* to do," she said gently.

He was silent for a long, long time. Faith chewed on her lower lip and fidgeted. His entire well-being, and possibly their future together, hinged on this moment, and she had to resist the urge to shake some understanding into Jones. The truth seemed so plain to her. But then, she'd had weeks of convalescence to figure it out. Jones had had only one day.

When he spoke again, he did so slowly, cautiously. "I could open my own practice, I suppose. Rent a little office right there in Holland."

"Do you think you'd like that?"

"Oh, yeah," he answered without hesitation. "I enjoy practicing law. It's those big, high-pressure bank cases with hours in the courtroom and millions riding on my every word that I can't stand. I like dealing with people, helping them solve their problems. And I like the idea of being my own boss."

"Running your own business can be pretty hairy," Faith cautioned.

"It couldn't be any more stressful than the alternative," he murmured. "Estate planning, family law, an occasional traffic ticket—yeah, I'd like that. I could take on the cases I like and turn down the others. Isn't that one of the keys to avoiding stress? Having control?"

"I believe so."

"I could keep the cabin at Caddo and go there on weekends. Then, anytime I started to get headaches, I could just clear my schedule and hibernate there until I feel better. Although maybe I wouldn't get headaches anymore.''

The more he talked, the more animated he became. Their quarrel was forgotten, for the moment, as he spun out a fantasy future. It didn't escape Faith that she didn't seem to be playing a part in it. But the important thing was that he'd made a breakthrough in his thinking. He'd recognized the harmful pattern in his life—the fact that he'd always done what was expected rather than what would make him happy.

He looked up suddenly, fixing Faith with a gaze that made her feel like a butterfly pinned to a board. ''I almost forgot the whole reason we got into this discussion,'' he said. ''I think I see, now, why you don't want to marry me. You fell in love with a laid-back fisherman, and suddenly I was turning into a stressed-out lawyer.''

''Something like that,'' she mumbled.

''Do you think you could settle for something in between?''

He was so damn sincere, and it was tearing her up inside. ''I think you missed the point,'' she said evenly. ''You don't want to be married. Your body told you that.''

''My body...'' He thought for a minute. ''Oh, I get it. Being engaged is part of what made me sick.''

She nodded miserably.

''You're partly right. True, every time I thought about that wedding I got a sick feeling in the pit of my stomach. But that's because I was engaged to Mary-Lynn, and I wasn't in love with her.

''This is completely different. I'm in love with you. Loving you has healed me, it's made me whole again. You're my reason for being, for *living*, and I can't think of anything healthier than marrying you.''

"But..." Her objection died stillborn. Could he be right, or was he just rationalizing? Could she afford to believe him? Hope flared inside her so brightly it nearly burned her.

He continued, undaunted. "If you're worried that a long engagement will get on my nerves, I have a solution to that. We'll elope. We'll fly to Vegas."

She was utterly speechless. The man was mad as a hatter. But his enthusiasm was infectious, and suddenly she found herself seriously considering his outrageous plan, daring to dream the impossible.

He folded her hands in his. "It's not that I don't believe we have a long, long life together ahead of us, but there's something to be said for living for the moment, enjoying the here and now. We've both learned to do that, right?"

She nodded uncertainly.

"Then let's do it. Let's drive to the airport and hop the first plane to Vegas with two empty seats. I love you, Faith, and I want you with me the rest of my life, regardless of whether that life is a few weeks or a hundred years. I've never been more sure of anything."

Whatever doubts she'd had evaporated when she looked into his eyes and saw the absolute commitment and unmitigated love residing there. Although it was dark outside, and the only light in the room was a dim bulb from a table lamp, for the first time she saw Jones standing in full, bright sunlight, just as she had dreamed she would all those weeks ago.

"Okay," she said, just like that.

He grinned and kissed her, a sweet, gentle embrace that spoke of a love so pure she wanted to drown in it. Then he pulled away, his hazel eyes full of mischief. He looked as happy and carefree as she'd ever seen him. It was hard to

believe he was the same man who had threatened to chase
her off his island with a gun.

"You'll pack that black silky thing, won't you?" he
asked, playfully dipping one finger down the front of her
shirt.

Within five minutes they were walking out the door,
hastily packed bags in hand, heading into their future.

Epilogue

Faith sat on the cabin's front steps, watching as the morning sun burned up the last of the damp fog. She loved this part of the day best, watching the world come awake before the summer heat drove her indoors. Her two-month-old daughter gurgled as she nursed, and a familiar sense of contentment stole over Faith. In the two years since she and Jones had married in a ridiculously tawdry but breathlessly romantic ceremony, she'd had no cause to look back or regret a single action.

In the distance a movement caught her eye. A formless shadow cut through the mist, eventually emerging and taking on the distinctive shape of a hefty woman paddling a canoe.

Faith gasped. *Miss Hildy!* The old medicine woman had disappeared last fall without a word. Faith and Jones had both feared the worst.

Faith laid the baby on her quilt-covered pallet, then scampered down the stairs to meet the canoe. "Miss Hildy!" she cried as she guided the boat onto shore, soaking her tennis shoes. "Where have you been? We've both been worried sick about you." Before Hildy was even out of the canoe Faith gave her an enthusiastic hug, nearly sending them both crashing into the shallow water.

"Land sakes, child, don't have a fit. Can't a body take a little vacation without everybody making a ruckus about it?"

"A vacation? You've been gone for months and months! Why didn't you tell us?" Faith asked as they made their way toward the cabin.

"Well, I was afraid I would chicken out, and then I'd feel like a fool. I went to Mexico for the winter and stayed on longer than I'd planned."

"Mexico!" Faith stopped in her tracks. "But I thought you never—"

"I never did, till now. But it's a place I've always dreamed about. I've been saving my money, but, truth is, it took me thirty years to find the courage to go. I figured, if Jones can do it, if he can leave the swamp, so can I."

Faith was flabbergasted. "That's wonderful! Did you like it?"

"I did. The things they grow down there! I set up a vegetable stand, and in three months I paid for the whole trip. I may do it again next year." She perused Faith from head to toe. "You've filled out some."

Faith patted her stomach self-consciously. It was far from flat, but her muscle tone improved every day. She took Hildy's hand. "Come on, there's someone you have to meet."

Hildy gave a crow of delight when she spied the infant dozing on her pallet. "Oh, just look at her, she's adorable. Can I hold her?"

Faith picked up the baby and handed her to Hildy, who cuddled her with a surprising amount of maternal skill.

"She's beautiful. What's her name?"

"Well, her father wanted to name her Hildy—"

"Pshaw, why would you saddle a little mite like this with such an ugly name?" she asked as they all settled onto the steps, but her eyes shone at the mere suggestion just the same. "I imagine you nixed that idea in a hurry."

"Not me, but her Grandmother Jones thought the baby should be named after a family member. Hers, naturally. But if we did that, *my* mother would get her feelings hurt, and I couldn't see using both names. Helen Ellen Jones just doesn't sound good."

Hildy chuckled. "How much longer is this story going to drag on?"

"All right, all right. To keep the peace, Jones and I gave the baby her very own name, one she wouldn't have to share with anyone. Rachel."

Hildy smiled her approval as she jiggled the baby and got a smile out of her. "It suits. Speaking of Jones, how's he doing?"

"Couldn't be better. His practice is booming. Sometimes I have to drag him away from his desk." Usually it wasn't too hard. When she thought he was working too much, she would call him and mention something about black lace, and he would be home in ten minutes.

"No more headaches?"

"Hardly ever."

"And you? How's your teachin'?"

"Nonexistent, thank goodness." It had taken her a year to find a suitable position within commuting distance of

Holland, at Baylor University in Waco. She'd liked it at first, but then she'd gotten pregnant and she'd found out just how narrow-minded all of her male colleagues could be about the possibility of juggling family and career. Seeing the long, uphill battle she faced, she'd opted out of the high-pressure environment.

"But what about your anther-pology?" Hildy asked. "You haven't given that up, have you?"

"Oh, no. I'll be teaching some classes at the junior college in Holland starting next year, and I'm looking forward to that. The schedule won't be nearly as demanding, and the school is only a ten-minute drive from home."

Miss Hildy nodded. Then she asked in a low voice, "How are the in-laws? Still giving you trouble?"

Faith laughed at Hildy's ominous tone. "Rachel's appearance has changed their attitudes considerably. You should see Helen goo-gooing over her grandbaby. Completely undignified. And she didn't say a word when the baby threw up on her Bill Blass suit. I think she may finally forgive us for eloping."

Even Mary-Lynn had become a friend. She and Faith had given birth to their firstborns within two weeks of each other, and, since they lived almost next door—Holland was not a big town—they had commiserated over diapers and 2:00 a.m. feedings. Mary-Lynn was, in fact, a sensitive and caring person, if a tad overdramatic, and Faith had come to like her a lot. It was easy to see why Jones hadn't wanted to hurt her.

The front door opened, and Faith turned to see her husband stumble outside, still groggy from sleep. She enjoyed watching his reaction when he realized who was sitting there on the steps holding his baby. He actually rubbed his eyes and looked again.

"Miss Hildy!"

Hildy handed the baby to Faith, then lumbered to her feet and gave Jones a bone-crushing hug. "There you are, you good-lookin' son-of-a-gun," she said. "I was just getting acquainted with your daughter."

Jones pulled up a deck chair and joined them, eager to hear the story of what had happened to Hildy over the winter. As she recounted the tale, with more relish and detail this time, Faith leaned back and thought about deep things, like how one impulsive act of heroism could change so many lives.

If Jones hadn't pulled her from that burning car, she wouldn't be alive today. If she hadn't gone looking for him, if she hadn't stood up to his intimidation tactics, he might still be living here alone, brooding in silence and misery. If Miss Hildy hadn't cared enough to bare her soul to Faith and encourage her to persevere, she might have left Caddo Lake forever. And if Jones hadn't found the courage to face those doctors and their tests, Miss Hildy might never have found her own courage.

Rachel had fallen asleep, and Jones absently reached for her. He loved to hold her and take care of her. Now he cradled the baby in his lap with infinite tenderness, the best, most doting father any child could want. If not for the love Faith and Jones had found, Rachel wouldn't exist.

"Faith, are you crying?" Jones asked suddenly.

She quickly blinked back the moisture as she gave his hand a reassuring squeeze. "Just the sun in my eyes," she said. Full, bright sun.

*   *   *   *   *

SILHOUETTE®
Desire®

MAN of the Month
1994

They're the hottest books around...

With heroes you've grown to know—and *love*...

Created by Top authors—the ones *you* say are your favorites...

MAN OF THE MONTH: 1994

Don't miss a single one of these handsome hunks—

In January
Secret Agent Man
by *Diana Palmer*

In February
Wild Innocence
by *Ann Major*

In March
Wrangler's Lady
by *Jackie Merritt*

In April
Bewitched
by *Jennifer Greene*

In May
Lucy and the Stone
by *Dixie Browning*

In June
Haven's Call
by *Robin Elliott*

And that's just the first six months! Later in the year, look for books by Joan Hohl, Barbara Boswell, Cait London and Annette Broadrick.

Man of the Month...only from Silhouette Desire

MOM94JJ

Take 4 bestselling love stories FREE

Plus get a FREE surprise gift!

Special Limited-time Offer

Mail to Silhouette Reader Service™

3010 Walden Avenue
P.O. Box 1867
Buffalo, N.Y. 14269-1867

YES! Please send me 4 free Silhouette Desire® novels and my free surprise gift. Then send me 6 brand-new novels every month, which I will receive months before they appear in bookstores. Bill me at the low price of $2.44 each plus 25¢ delivery and applicable sales tax, if any.* That's the complete price and—compared to the cover prices of $2.99 each—quite a bargain! I understand that accepting the books and gift places me under no obligation ever to buy any books. I can always return a shipment and cancel at any time. Even if I never buy another book from Silhouette, the 4 free books and the surprise gift are mine to keep forever.

225 BPA ANRS

Name	(PLEASE PRINT)	
Address	Apt. No.	
City	State	Zip

This offer is limited to one order per household and not valid to present Silhouette Desire® subscribers. *Terms and prices are subject to change without notice.
Sales tax applicable in N.Y.

UDES-94R   ©1990 Harlequin Enterprises Limited

SPRING

fancy

'94

**They're sexy, single...
and about to get snagged!**

Passion is in full bloom as love catches
the fancy of three brash bachelors. You won't
want to miss these stories by three of
Silhouette's hottest authors:

CAIT LONDON
DIXIE BROWNING
PEPPER ADAMS

Spring fever is in the air this March—
and there's no avoiding it!

Only from 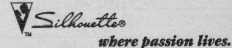 *Silhouette®*

where passion lives.

**It's our 1000th
Silhouette Romance
and we're celebrating!**

Join us for a special collection of love stories by the authors you've loved for years, and new favorites you've just discovered.

**It's a celebration just for you,
with wonderful books by
Diana Palmer, Suzanne Carey,
Tracy Sinclair, Marie Ferrarella,
Debbie Macomber, Laurie Paige,
Annette Broadrick, Elizabeth August
and MORE!**

Silhouette Romance...vibrant, fun and emotionally rich! Take another look at us!

As part of the celebration, readers can receive a FREE gift AND enter our exciting sweepstakes to win a grand prize of $1000! Look for more details in all March Silhouette series titles.

**You'll fall in love all over again
with Silhouette Romance!**

As seen on TV!
Free Gift Offer

With a Free Gift proof-of-purchase from any Silhouette® book,
you can receive a beautiful cubic zirconia pendant.

This gorgeous marquise-shaped stone is a genuine cubic
zirconia—accented by an 18" gold tone necklace.
(Approximate retail value $19.95)

Send for yours today...
compliments of ▼ *Silhouette*®
™

To receive your free gift, a cubic zirconia pendant, send us one original proof-of-
purchase, photocopies not accepted, from the back of any Silhouette Romance™,
Silhouette Desire®, Silhouette Special Edition®, Silhouette Intimate Moments® or
Silhouette Shadows™ title for January, February or March 1994 at your favorite retail
outlet, together with the Free Gift Certificate, plus a check or money order for $2.50
(do not send cash) to cover postage and handling, payable to Silhouette Free Gift Offer.
We will send you the specified gift. Allow 6 to 8 weeks for delivery. Offer good until
March 31st, 1994 or while quantities last. Offer valid in the U.S. and Canada only.

Free Gift Certificate

Name: _____

Address: _____

City: _____ State/Province: _____ Zip/Postal Code: _____

Mail this certificate, one proof-of-purchase and a check or money order for postage
and handling to: SILHOUETTE FREE GIFT OFFER 1994. In the U.S.: 3010 Walden
Avenue, P.O. Box 9057, Buffalo NY 14269-9057. In Canada: P.O. Box 622, Fort Erie,
Ontario L2Z 5X3

FREE GIFT OFFER   079-KBZ
ONE PROOF-OF-PURCHASE
To collect your fabulous FREE GIFT, a cubic zirconia pendant, you must include this
original proof-of-purchase for each gift with the properly completed Free Gift Certificate.

079-KBZ